SOMEPLACE *to* CALL HOME

Someplace to Call Home

by Sandra Dallas

PUBLISHED *by* SLEEPING BEAR PRESS

Sleeping Bear Press™

2395 South Huron Parkway, Suite 200, Ann Arbor, MI 48104
www.sleepingbearpress.com
© Sleeping Bear Press

Printed and bound in the United States.

Library of Congress Cataloging-in-Publication Data
Names: Dallas, Sandra, author.
Title: Someplace to call home / written by Sandra Dallas.
Description: Ann Arbor, MI : Sleeping Bear Press, [2019] | Summary:
In 1933, when twelve-year-old Hallie Turner and her brothers,
Tom and Benny, take to the road seeking whatever work they
can get, they find kindness in small-townAnsas.
Identifiers: LCCN 2019004065
ISBN 978-1-58536-414-5 (hc) 10 9 8 7 6 5 4
ISBN 978-1-58536-415-2 (pbk) 10 9 8 7 6 5 4 3
Subjects: LCSH: Dust Bowl Era, 1931-1939--Juvenile fiction.
Depressions--1929--Juvenile fiction. | CYAC: Dust Bowl Era,
1931-1939--Fiction. | Depressions--1929--Fiction. | Brothers and
sisters--Fiction. | Orphans--Fiction. | Poverty--Fiction.
Classification: LCC PZ7.D1644 So 2019 | DDC [Fic]--dc23
LC record available at https://lccn.loc.gov/2019004065

This is for Forrest Athearn and for his great-grandfather,

Forrest Dallas

—SANDRA

Broken Down

The battered old Model T Ford sputtered and stalled. With a sigh, sixteen-year-old Tom Turner guided it to the side of the dirt road. He slid out of the worn seat on the driver's side and stood next to the vehicle, stopping a moment as he heard a hissing sound. He shook his head. "The transmission's bad, and it looks like we blew a tire, too."

Hallie Turner took a deep breath. "As Mommy used to say, if it's not one thing, it's another. More bad luck."

"Not so bad," Tom said. He pointed to a grove of trees. "If we had to break down, at least we found a nice shady spot."

Hallie glanced around. She said to the little boy on the

seat beside her, "Look, Benny, there's a stream."

Benny brightened. "I like water," he said. He slid over the seat, jumping out on the driver's side. He had been sitting between Hallie and Tom.

"Careful, Benny," Hallie called. She watched her little brother run toward the water.

"Don't worry. It looks like there's not but a trickle of water in it," Tom told her.

"That's good. You know how he is with water. He could drown in a tin cup."

Hallie opened the passenger door of the Tin Lizzie and got out. She looked around. It was indeed a pretty spot—the trees, the stream, and a patch of yellow dandelions nodding in the sun. She stretched and dug her bare toes into the dirt. She shook her dress, which was covered with dust that had blown in through the open window.

The car, too, was covered with grime. The whole world except for this little spot seemed to be dirty. When the dust had gotten too bad, Hallie had rolled up the car windows and stuffed rags where they didn't quite close. That didn't stop the dirt from blowing in. She had to wipe the inside of the car clean every night. "I guess if the car's broke down, we'll be staying for a spell," she said. She grasped the handle of the door to close it and quickly removed her hand. She should have known better than to touch the metal. It was burning hot from the sun.

"We don't have much choice. I can patch the tire again." Tom glanced at the tire that seemed to be more patches than tire. "But we'll have to replace the transmission. How much money do we have left?"

"Four dollars and twelve cents." Hallie didn't have to look into the ragged coin purse. She knew to the penny how much was in it.

"Not enough for the transmission. I'll have to find work."

Hallie laughed. "Where are you going to do that? We've tried everywhere. Not more than two days' work in the field in the past two weeks. If we hadn't found those tomatoes last week, we'd be eating grass."

She thought of the deserted house they'd stopped at with three perfectly good tomato plants loaded with fruit. She shook her head at the wonder of it. They guessed the farmer had been dusted out. That's what folks said when the dust storms destroyed crops, forcing farmers to desert their homes. Somehow the tomato plants had thrived. They were all tired of tomatoes by now, but they were grateful for them nonetheless.

"That was good luck, all right. Maybe our luck's changed."

"I wouldn't call a busted transmission good luck," Hallie told her brother.

"I guess you're right about that." Tom went back to the Ford. "I'd best unload this old Tin Lizzie. You look after Benny." Tom stood next to the open lid of the car's rumble seat. He began taking out boxes containing quilts and blankets, a tarp, a collection of pots and pans, and a few dishes. "Where should I put these?"

Hallie looked about. Then she pointed to a secluded spot hidden by trees. "We don't want anyone seeing us from the road," she said. Of course, anybody driving by would notice the car. Maybe they'd think it was abandoned. The flivver was that old and dilapidated. Tom had had to remove the leather bench in the rumble seat to make room for their belongings, to Benny's disappointment. He had loved to ride in the back in the open air. Now Tom spread the tarp on the ground. Next, he removed two thin mattresses tied to the roof of the car and laid them on top of the tarp.

Hallie watched him, then turned back to Benny. The six-year-old was sitting beside the stream. Every now and then, he stuck his foot into the water, then pulled it back and laughed. "I'm wet," he said.

Hallie went to the creek and tickled his toes. She thought what a happy, good-natured boy he was.

"I like water, Hallie," he said again.

Hallie scooped up a handful of water and sprinkled it on Benny's head. He giggled. "That will cool you off," she said. She splashed water over her arms and legs, too. Despite the shade of the trees, she was hot. It seemed it was always hot in Kansas. In Oklahoma, too. She couldn't remember the last time it had rained.

"I want my boat," Benny said. The boat was his favorite toy.

Hallie went to a box that Tom had set down. She rummaged through it until she found a battered wooden boat. Tom had carved it and painted it, too. The paint was mostly worn off now. "You play with it while I help Tom," she told Benny.

She stretched to get the kinks out of her back. Hallie wasn't just hot. She was tired from riding for days down the dirt roads looking for work. Tom had stopped at farms, asking if anyone needed help. No one did. Crops were poor because of the drought. Farmworkers were plentiful. Many farmers couldn't pay for hired help even if they needed it. Those who could pay wanted grown men. "Me and my sister can do the work of two men and be paid half as much," Tom would tell the farmers. The Turners still couldn't find employment.

A few of the farmers they had approached ran them off as if they'd been homeless dogs. Most were sympathetic, however. "I'd like to help, but I don't have the money to pay you. You come around next year. Maybe 1934 will be better," one farmer had told them.

His wife had come outside with a dishpan of water. She threw it on a flower bed, then looked them over. "Why, honey, they ain't nothing but kids," she told her husband. "Where's your folks at, kids?"

Tom and Hallie didn't answer. The woman shrugged. "You ain't the first orphans that's come around. You sit down and have you a glass of cold buttermilk before you go on. That's the least we can do." She turned to her husband. "Folks is one after another coming down that road looking for work. Times is sure hard." She went inside and returned with a pitcher of buttermilk and three glasses and handed them around. She stared at Benny but didn't say anything.

When the three had finished drinking, Hallie rinsed off the glasses at the pump. She set them beside the back porch steps. The woman had gone inside, so Hallie told the man, "We sure are obliged to you."

"I wish I could hire you . . . ," he said.

"We understand," Tom told him. He and Hallie and Benny had climbed back into the car and headed for the next farm.

"We'll find something. We always do," Hallie said now as she helped Tom with the boxes. She was right. Just when things seemed hardest, Tom got a half-day's work for fifty cents. Then they'd found those tomatoes. Until then, they'd been eating pancakes made from flour and water. They'd paid a nickel for a half-dozen eggs to mix with the pancake batter, but Benny had dropped the eggs on the ground, and they'd broken.

Now she glanced at where Benny sat playing with the boat. "You stay there, Benny. Don't go off."

They had to watch Benny all the time. It wasn't that

he didn't mind them. He was easily distracted. He would see a bird far off and run to it, calling, "Hi, bird." Or he'd discover a flower. He'd pick it for Hallie, then spot another one farther away. Whenever he saw a rabbit, he called, "Hi, Bob." He'd follow it until the rabbit disappeared. Back in Oklahoma, he'd had a pet rabbit named Bob. Now each time he caught sight of a rabbit, he thought it was his friend and would try to catch it.

Of course, it was hard having to take care of a six-year-old. Hallie and Tom might have been hired more often if they hadn't had the little boy to take care of. Even as a twelve-year-old, Hallie had had a few offers for work. A woman wanted to pay her a quarter to clean her house. She'd brought Benny with her. The woman had said she wouldn't allow the boy inside. Hallie couldn't leave Benny outside by himself. So she'd had to turn down the job. She might have been resentful of Benny, but she wasn't. She and Tom loved their little brother and protected him fiercely.

Tom gathered rocks and made a circle. Then he collected wood for a fire. They were careful about camping. When they left a campsite, they always put out the fire. They also returned the rocks to where they'd been. "It's the least we can do," Tom said. "We're trespassing on someone's land, even if the owners have been dusted out and moved on."

The fire Tom built made Hallie even hotter. Of course, they didn't need the fire to keep warm. They needed it to cook the tomatoes, which were mushy now. At first, Hallie had cut them in half and they'd eaten them with salt. After a few days, they were so soft that they had to be cooked. The night before, she had made a tomato stew, adding chunks of bread to the pot with the stewed tomatoes. The bread was gone. So she mixed up biscuits, using flour, baking powder, water, and a pinch of salt, while she decided what to do with the tomatoes. "How about tomato soup for supper?" she called to Benny.

"No more tomatoes," he replied.

Hallie, too, was tired of tomatoes, but there was nothing else to eat, except for biscuits. Besides, she wouldn't throw away perfectly good food, even if they were sick of it. She thought a moment, then said, "Then how about red soup, Benny? You like red."

"I like red," he agreed.

Hallie smiled at the boy while she dumped the last of the tomatoes into an old pot, blackened from use. She smashed them into a pulp with a potato masher. She went to the stream and using a tin can, dipped up water to add to the soup, then set the pot on the fire Tom had built.

As the soup heated, she spread quilts on top of the mattresses. Her mother had made some of them from patches cut from men's worn-out jackets and pants. They were as heavy as the iron that Hallie had once heated on the cook stove back in Oklahoma to iron clothes. Sleeping under those quilts was like sleeping under a pile of cast-iron stove lids. They'd been grateful for them in the winter, but they didn't need their warmth now. The three would sleep on top of them. She set Benny's pillow on the mattress he shared with Tom. She was glad one of the pillows had survived. Two had blown off the top of the car. They hadn't known of the loss until they stopped to camp. Hallie went back to the fire. The soup was scorched, and she added more water, then stirred the burned bits into the soup. She made coffee by pouring water into the coffeepot, which held the grounds left over from the day before. They used the grounds three or four times before throwing them out. When all was ready, she called, "Supper!"

"Oh boy, red soup," said Tom, who had heard the

exchange between his sister and brother.

"Oh boy," Benny repeated as he watched Hallie pour the soup into his tin cup.

He put the cup to his mouth to drink it, but Hallie handed him a spoon. "We use a spoon for soup. We have to mind our manners even when we're camping," she said. "And we have to give thanks."

"Okay," Benny told her. He bowed his head while Hallie said grace. Then he ate the soup quickly and said, "Good red soup."

Tom and Hallie smiled at each other over the little boy's head. "It is good red soup," Tom said.

"More," Benny said.

"That's all there is." Hallie handed Benny a biscuit. He took it and stood up and went back to his boat.

"That's it?" Tom asked.

Hallie knew he wanted more, too. He was hungry. He was always hungry. So was she.

"That's the last of the tomatoes," she said. "From now on, it's back to beans or pancakes."

Tom nodded. "There must be a town down the road. I'll walk there tomorrow and see if I can find a job. You stay here with Benny."

"Maybe you can get work at a filling station. Maybe somebody needs a car fixed." Tom knew everything about cars. That was why he knew that the transmission needed to be replaced. He'd nursed it along for days.

"Maybe," he said.

Or maybe not, Hallie thought. She tried to be upbeat with her brothers, but at heart, she worried. It wasn't fair, the fix they were in. They'd had the worst luck. She felt discouraged sometimes until she realized that others had the worst luck, too. It wasn't just the dust storms, with farms drying up and blowing away. There was also the depression. Thousands of men all over the country were out of work. Hallie and Tom had driven through Oklahoma City and Kansas City and Topeka and had seen folks in bread lines waiting for free government food. "Should we stop and join them?" Tom asked. After all, they needed the food.

Hallie wouldn't let him join the line. "There are others who are needier than us," she told him. Tom had nodded and driven on. They had had a meager supper that night. Since then, there'd been many suppers like it.

Hallie hated their situation, but it didn't do any good

to complain. She went to the stream to wash the dishes, then played with Benny and his boat. Tom replaced rocks that had slid down the bank into the water and cleaned out deadwood that clogged the campsite.

Later Tom joined his brother and sister. "I've been looking around. There's an old cabin over yonder. It looks like nobody's lived there in a long time. We're going to be here awhile. Maybe we could move in there."

Hallie shook her head. "It doesn't belong to us."

"We'd leave it better than we found it. I was just thinking—"

"It wouldn't be right, Tom."

Her brother nodded. Although Hallie was four years younger than Tom, when she put her foot down, he didn't oppose her. Her final argument was always, "It wouldn't be right."

Instead he said, "Maybe I should put up the tent." He had left the tent on top of the Model T. It was old and worn and filled with rips that Hallie had sewn up. There were so many tears and zigzagged seams that the tent looked like one of the crazy quilts Mommy had made.

"Why?" Hallie asked. "It's too hot to sleep in the tent."

"We'll have to be here for a few days. What if it rains?"

"Rains? If it rains, we'll all stand outside and praise the Lord. When was the last time you saw rain, Tom?"

"Let's see." Tom tilted his head, thinking. "I think it was in 1929. The Bible says we have seven good years and seven bad, so we should have rain in two or three years."

"Well, I hope the Lord can count," Hallie told him. She stared at her brother until the two burst out laughing. She felt good finding something funny.

It was dusk now. Benny lay down on one of the quilts. "Are we home, Hallie?" he asked.

She shook her head.

"I know, let's sing a song," Benny begged.

"What song, Benny?"

"The happy song." They had heard "Happy Days Are Here Again" on the radio at home, and Benny loved it. Often at night around a campfire, the three of them sang "You Are My Sunshine" and "When You Wore a Tulip." Benny always wanted the happy song before he went to sleep.

Hallie began singing the words. Tom joined her, pretending he was strumming a guitar. Benny chimed in, making up the words as he went along.

Suddenly Tom stopped. Hallie looked up at him, then realized her brother was staring at something behind her. She turned and saw a man walking through the black trees toward them, a shotgun in his arms.

We're Not Squatters

The man was tall and lean with a thin nose. He had a hard look on his face. The light had faded to dusk. Hallie couldn't make out his eyes, whether they were kind or mean. He held the gun lightly, but she knew he could cock and fire it before Tom could pick up a rock and throw it at him. She was afraid of guns. Tom had wanted to bring their shotgun with them, but Hallie said it would only cause trouble. Tom had argued that he could shoot rabbits for food, but Hallie knew that would upset Benny. The little boy would believe Tom had killed Bob. "Guns are just trouble," she'd said. She was so fierce about leaving the gun behind that Tom had not taken it. Now as she saw the gun in the man's hand, Hallie wondered if she had been wrong. Maybe they needed a gun to protect themselves.

She went over and stood next to Tom. She knew why the man was there. They had camped on his land. He had come to tell them to get off. "I hope he'll let us stay till morning," she whispered to her brother.

They had been threatened before. People, sometimes with guns or sticks, had called them squatters. Hallie hated the word. It meant down-and-outers who "squatted" on private land. Sometimes squatters were people who robbed and left their campsites full of debris when they pulled out. Hallie and Tom weren't like that. They couldn't help that they were poor. They didn't deserve to be treated like trash. When they camped on private land, they made sure their fire was extinguished before they left. They used a tree branch to sweep the ground, removing traces of their camp. They "paid" for their stay by leaving the site better than they'd found it. Tom had rebuilt a rock wall once. Hallie and Benny had weeded a flower patch.

Tom didn't move forward, didn't hold out his hand. He stood there for a moment, staring at the man. When the man didn't speak, Tom finally said, "Evening, sir."

The man didn't reply. He glanced around the camp.

"We got a little coffee left. It ain't fresh made, but it's only a day or two old. We'd be proud to share it with you," Tom said.

"Already had my coffee," the man replied. "I seen smoke."

"We've been careful with the fire, mister," Hallie spoke up. "We're always careful about fires. Why, you can see we put rocks around where we set it. We'll pour water over the coals and even kick dirt over them when we're done to make sure the fire's out. There's no cause to worry. We're responsible."

"Ain't just the fire. You're squatting on private land. *My* land."

Hallie flinched at the word and began to protest that they weren't squatters, but Tom held up his hand to still her. "We just want the borrow of this place for a few days. We'll be moving on directly," he said. "We expect to leave your land better than we found it. I already shored up the stream bank and cleaned up some brush. We're fixing to burn it."

"Didn't ask you to."

"No," Tom said.

"Didn't think to ask if you could trespass, did you?"

"I didn't know who to ask," Tom replied.

They hadn't wanted to ask, Hallie knew. They might have been turned down.

"You can stay the night. I'll expect you gone by sunup."

"The thing is, we can't move on tomorrow," Tom said. "That's our automobile over there. It's got a flat tire, and the transmission's bad. You don't know where I can get one, do you? For less than four dollars?"

"Don't know about cars. We got enough trouble with a broke tractor needs fixing. I can't figure what's wrong."

Tom grinned. "I could take a look at it. I'm real good at motors. I worked in a garage in Cookietown, Oklahoma, till we got dusted out."

"Oklahoma, that where you from? You're Okies, then?"

"And proud of it," Hallie spoke up. "We had a house and farm and even a radio."

"Well, I would like to hear a radio. Radio's busted up as bad as the tractor."

"Tom could fix that, too," Hallie told him.

"You're just an all-around fix-it man, ain't you, boy?"

Tom didn't reply.

The man was quiet, too. Then he said, "The wife would like to hear that radio again. My girl, too."

"I could take a look at it," Tom said again.

"Naw, the wife won't let you in the house." He looked Tom up and down. "But I could let you see about the tractor. What you going to charge me?"

Tom shook his head. "Not a thing. I'll do it as payment for letting us camp here."

"I couldn't do that. Camping don't cost me nothing. It wouldn't be right to charge you."

Hallie liked that the man said "it wouldn't be right."

"I'll pay you fifty cents," he said.

"Deal," Tom told him. He held out his hand. "I'm Tom Turner."

"Swede Carlson." The man shook Tom's hand.

"I'm Hazel Rose Turner, but everybody calls me Hallie," Hallie said.

"Pleased to meet you, Miss Hallie."

Benny, who had been lying down on the quilt almost asleep, stood up and said, "Hi, I'm Benny." He held out his hand, too.

Mr. Carlson stared at Benny for a long time.

Hallie and Tom exchanged a glance. They knew Benny was different. Hallie had known it the first time she held the boy after he was born. His face wasn't like other babies' faces. As he grew older, he didn't seem to learn as quickly as other children. Benny didn't speak clearly, and he didn't always understand things. But he had the sweetest disposition of any child they knew. Hallie thought he was a special gift. Benny was used to people staring at him. Sometimes they called him stupid or a dummy, which upset him. A few were afraid of him, as if Benny had some disease they could catch. She hoped Mr. Carlson wasn't that way. They needed the fifty cents for fixing the tractor.

After a time, Mr. Carlson smiled and took Benny's hand. "Hi, Benny," he said. "You look like a nice little boy."

"I am," Benny said.

Hallie realized she had been holding her breath. She let it out in a sigh of relief. She decided she liked Mr. Carlson.

"You two got you any other kids?" he asked.

Hallie laughed at that. "Tom's my brother. So's Benny."

"Where's your folks at?"

Tom looked off into the distance. He got choked up when people asked that. So Hallie answered. "They're gone." She hoped Mr. Carlson wouldn't ask for details. Daddy had taken off looking for work two years before and had never come back. Their sister, Barbara, had died of dust pneumonia. Then Mommy had grieved herself to death. Hallie and Tom had tried to farm the land by themselves after that, but with the drought, they couldn't make a go of it. They couldn't pay the mortgage. The bank had taken back the farm. They had had to move out.

"You and Benny could stay in an orphanage," Tom had told Hallie. "They won't take me because I'm too old, but you can go."

Hallie had refused. "They might be mean to Benny. Besides, I'm old enough to be on my own with you. Nobody cares. There are too many orphans in that place already. They don't want any more. We'll find a place to settle down, just the three of us."

An aunt, their father's sister, had offered to take Benny. She threatened to go to court to get custody of the boy if Tom and Hallie wouldn't give him up. Hallie knew the aunt didn't love Benny the way they did. She believed the woman wanted Benny only because her own little boy had died. Tom and Hallie refused. They sold off Mommy's china dishes and the bureau that had belonged to their grandmother. Hallie gave away most of the fine quilts and the rag carpet. Then they packed up what would fit into the Model T and left Cookietown. That was in December, eight months ago, but the hurt was still raw. Hallie wanted to cry every time she thought of her mother and her pretty younger sister. She'd kept Mommy's silver wedding ring and Barbara's hair ribbons, but she couldn't look at them. They made her cry. She tried hard not to show Tom and Benny how much she missed Mommy and Barbara.

At first, Tom had wanted to go to California to pick oranges. Then they heard that people in California didn't want Okies and were trying to keep them out. Besides, Hallie wanted a place to settle down. She wanted to make a home for Benny. She also dreamed of finishing eighth grade, like Tom had. But things hadn't worked out that way. Because they were on the road, Hallie no longer attended school, and there was no full-time employment for Tom. It was likely the three of them would be roaming Oklahoma and Kansas and living out of their car for a long time.

Mr. Carlson didn't pursue an answer to his question about their family. The drought had created other orphans.

Perhaps he'd seen them. Instead, he asked, "You young folks planning on going back to Oklahoma?"

"Maybe if it rains and the dust settles," Tom told him.

"I guess it's pretty bad down there. I heard of a fellow going along a road, dust so deep it was up to his neck. Neighbor comes past and says, 'Awful bad, ain't it?' The man tells him, 'Would be worse if I wasn't sitting on a horse.'" Mr. Carlson guffawed.

Tom slapped his knee with his hand. "That's a good one," he said, although he and Hallie had heard the story a dozen times.

Mr. Carlson pointed down the road to a farm that Hallie had noticed earlier. "You come on over to my place at sunup, and I'll show you that tractor." He nodded at Tom and Hallie, and then to their surprise, he took Benny's hand again and said, "I'm mighty proud to meet you, Benny."

⌒

Tom left early the next morning and was gone all day. When he returned, Hallie said, "That tractor must have been in pretty bad shape if it took you this long to fix it."

"Didn't take long at all. Mr. Carlson had me look over some of his other machinery. He's a good farmer, but he's not much of a hand at motors." Tom opened his hand. "He paid me a dollar."

"A dollar! For tinkering with motors?"

"He said it was worth every penny to him. I fixed the radio, too." Tom grinned at his sister. "And he wants me to come back tomorrow and help in the field."

"Tom, that's great!"

"Great," Benny repeated, although he didn't know what they were talking about.

"Tom's got work," Hallie told him.

"Great," Benny said again. "We found berries."

"We found a patch of blackberries," Hallie told Tom. "We'll have them with pancakes."

"No pancakes," Tom told her. "Look what I brought." He reached into his overalls front pocket and took out two pieces of fried chicken wrapped in wax paper. "Mrs. Carlson brought out dinner for us in the field. When I went to the house with Mr. Carlson to get my dollar, she told me to take the leftovers home with me. Mr. Carlson must have told her about you and Benny. I ate so much I'm hardly hungry." He handed the chicken to Hallie and Benny.

"I like chicken," Benny said.

"This is the best day since we found those tomatoes," Hallie said.

"It's even better than you think," Tom told her. "Just as I was leaving, Mrs. Carlson came outside and asked me if you'd like to help clean her house. She'll pay you a quarter. She said to bring Benny. I bet she'll fry another chicken."

Hallie stared at her brother. "If she'll fix us dinner, I'll work for free." She thought a moment. "But I'll still take the quarter." Then she asked, "What's their daughter like?"

Tom shook his head. "When I went inside to fix the radio, the girl was taking a nap. I didn't see her."

"I hope she's not mean to Benny." Just the week before, a boy had pointed at Benny and called him stupid.

That night, Hallie explained to Benny that she was taking him with her to Mr. Carlson's farm. She told him he must be a very good little boy and not get into things. "I'm good," he said.

"I know you are, Benny, but sometimes you forget." Then she said, "They have a girl there. Tom says her name is Tessie." She wanted to warn Benny that Tessie might not care to play with him, but she didn't want the little boy to worry. Maybe the girl was as nice as her parents.

———

Hallie herself worried about Tessie as she and Benny and Tom walked down the road to the Carlson farm. Benny was excited. He asked all about the girl, then declared, "Tessie's my friend."

"I hope so," Hallie told Tom. He was watching Benny kick a rock. Every now and then the boy stopped to study a bug or to pick the flowering weeds that grew along the roadside. Hallie had washed both Benny and herself. They'd dressed in clean clothes. She'd slicked back Benny's thick hair and braided her own. Still, she worried about what Mrs. Carlson would think of them. Their clothes were old. Benny's hands were dirty from picking the weeds. By the time they reached the Carlson place, Benny had a handful of the flowers.

Tom saw Mr. Carlson in the barn. He left Hallie and Benny by the back door of the house. Hallie knew better than to go to the front door. Front doors were for preachers and school teachers. She knocked on the door, then held her breath.

Mrs. Carlson looked a good deal like her husband, thin with a narrow face. She was only a little taller than Hallie, who was five feet, four inches the last time she measured. That was before they left Cookietown. She thought she was taller now, since the hem of her dress was above her knees.

Mrs. Carlson opened the screen door and looked Hallie and Benny up and down. Then she smiled and called, "Tessie, someone's come to play with you."

A little girl about Benny's size came outside and beamed at Benny. As much as she resented people staring at her little brother, Hallie couldn't help but gape at Tessie. The girl had Benny's same eyes and face, the same short neck and fingers. She glanced at Mrs. Carlson, who smiled at her.

Benny grinned. "She's pretty," he told Hallie. Then he held out the bouquet of weeds.

Mrs. Carlson put out her hand. "Why, thank you, Benny," she said.

"No," Benny said. "Not you. Tessie." He handed the bouquet to Tessie.

"What do you say?" Mrs. Carlson prodded her daughter.

"Thank you." She gave the flowers to her mother. "I have a swing."

"A swing!" Benny cried.

"You can push me. Come on."

"Okay." The two children ran off.

Hallie and Mrs. Carlson watched them for a moment. Then Hallie said, "I didn't know you had a girl like Benny."

"No. Mr. Carlson didn't say anything." Mrs. Carlson was silent for a moment. Hallie wondered if Mr. Carlson hadn't said anything because he wanted to see what kind of worker Tom was before he let Tessie meet Benny. The Carlsons might not have wanted to be friends with folks they thought were squatters.

"Do you think Tessie knows that Benny is . . . is like her?" Hallie asked. "Benny wouldn't know because he's never seen himself in a mirror."

"I don't know. She's just happy to have someone to play with. She's lonely. The other children . . . well, sometimes they don't like being around her. Tessie's such a sweet little girl, and children can say hurtful things. They don't mean to be cruel, of course, but they can be thoughtless."

"I know," Hallie said.

"Of course you do. Now come into the house. It's hot enough for the hens to lay hard-boiled eggs."

Hallie followed Mrs. Carlson inside, careful not to let the screen door bang. She looked around the kitchen in wonder. Instead of a pie safe, Mrs. Carlson had cupboards attached to the walls. "They keep the dust out," Mrs. Carlson said with a laugh. "With all the dirt flying around these days, I'd have had to wash the dishes before we ate as well as after."

There was a porcelain sink with running water, not a pump, and a real refrigerator with a motor on top, in place of an icebox. Best of all, there was a gas stove instead of a cook stove. It was white with black burners. Hallie had looked at pictures of such appliances but had never seen a real one. "Oh my," she said, staring at the stove.

"It's a beauty, isn't it?" Mrs. Carlson said. "Mr. Carlson bought it for me before the drought. Of course, after what's happened to the price of crops, it was foolish to spend so much for it. I'd sell it, but nobody's got the money to buy it." She grinned at Hallie. "It cooks awful good. To tell you the truth, I'm glad to have it instead of that old cook stove. I couldn't hardly stand to cook on it in this heat. The gas stove is so much safer for Tessie. I couldn't keep her away from the cook stove. I was afraid she'd burn herself."

Mrs. Carlson showed Hallie the rest of the house. There was a living room with a matching sofa and chair and the radio that Tom had fixed, and two bedrooms. The house even had a room just for Mrs. Carlson's sewing machine and fabric and patterns. Hallie thought it was the most beautiful house she'd ever seen and tried to picture herself living there. Tom and Benny would share one bedroom, and she would have a room of her own. She'd never imagined such a luxury. In Oklahoma, they had lived in a one-room house. Of course, Mommy had fixed it up nice, but it was still cramped. The children slept on mattresses on the floor. Mommy and Daddy had a curtained-off area to themselves. Hallie wondered if she'd ever have a home like the Carlsons'. *Will we ever have a home again?*

The Hired Man's Cabin

Benny sang a tuneless song as the three siblings walked back along the dusty road to where they had camped. He stopped to pick up a stick and dragged it in the dirt. "Tessie has a swing," he said. He'd told his brother about the swing three or four times already. "There's Bob!" he cried. A rabbit skittered through the bush beside them. "Hi, Bob." He watched the rabbit disappear. "I'll tell Tessie I saw Bob."

"Benny's had a good day," Tom told Hallie. "Maybe the best one since we left home."

"We've all had a good day," she replied. "I like helping Mrs. Carlson. It's fun. I decided not to take the quarter she offered. I feel I'm paying her back for letting us camp on their land. She said if I help her bottle tomatoes, she'll give me some."

"That's great. Mr. Carlson wants me to help him two days a week. He'll pay a dollar a day. He gave me a cartwheel for working today." Tom held out a silver dollar.

"Mr. Carlson's honest," Hallie said. "Still, I'm glad he'll pay you each time you work there." The month before, Tom had worked for a man who'd promised to pay him a dollar a day for five days' work, but later gave him only three. He said he was charging him for camping on his property.

"How was Mrs. Carlson?" Tom asked.

"We worked hard, but I didn't mind. Tom, I never knew about cleaning such a house. She has a carpet sweeper instead of a broom. It picks up dirt when you run it over a rug. When I washed her windows, I didn't use soap and water. Instead, she had me clean them with what she calls ammonia. When I was done, the glass just sparkled. She sprinkles Old Dutch cleanser on cooking pans. The burned places just come right off. You don't even have to scrape them. Can you imagine?" Hallie shook her head. "They sure are rich."

"You're not resentful, are you? Even rich folks are having

a hard time of it."

"Well, they're better off than we are."

"That's about right."

Hallie wondered if Tom was correct about her being resentful. Was she? Of course she was. It wasn't just the fancy stove and the carpet, the radio and the starched curtains. No, it was that the Carlsons had a home, a real home. The three of them had a house with beds and a kitchen table where they ate their meals. They didn't sleep on the ground. Nor did they cook their food over a campfire. Nobody was going to tell them to move along when they weren't needed anymore.

Still, she wasn't *real* jealous of them. Mrs. Carlson had been kind. She'd fixed ham sandwiches for everyone for dinner. Hallie had taken them along with a jug of water to Tom and Mr. Carlson in the field. When she returned, Mrs. Carlson had put a pretty tablecloth over the table. She had set china plates on it. Benny's bouquet of weeds sat in a glass of water at the center of the table. The sandwiches were the best Hallie had ever eaten, made with soft store-bought bread. There were two left over. Mrs. Carlson had insisted Hallie take them home for supper.

"How long are they going to let us camp here?" Hallie asked her brother.

Tom shrugged. "Mr. Carlson didn't say. But he didn't say we had to move on, either. I guess we can live here as long as he needs us."

"If he pays you two dollars a week, you'll have that new transmission in no time."

"Yeah, if we don't have to eat or buy clothes. Benny's grown out of his shoes. Yours are almost worn out."

"Other farmers might hire you when they see what a worker you are."

"We'll see. Mr. Carlson said he'll put my name out. He also said I should try at the garage in town, see if they need a mechanic. If they do, they'll probably hire somebody local, I'm afraid. People think of us as squatters. Still, I'll ask."

"Maybe we can stay here for a while, then."

"We'll have to move on before the weather turns. We can't live in a tent in the winter again or sleep in the car." They had left Oklahoma in the winter and had suffered from the cold. Benny had cried from it. Hallie knew she couldn't let the little boy go through that again. Perhaps they should go to California after all. It was August and hot weather. They wouldn't have to move on for a couple of months. In the meantime, she hoped they could stay on the Carlson land.

Hallie had been thinking about the Carlson house. She did not pay attention to the road until she turned to see a cloud of dust behind them and a car moving fast. Benny was squatting in the middle of the road with his stick. "Benny!" she called. Tom, too, spotted the auto and sprinted toward the little boy, grabbing him up.

The car screeched to a halt. It was a fancy car, a cream-colored convertible with big headlights on the front. Two boys about Tom's age were inside.

"You all right?" the passenger asked.

"Going pretty fast, aren't you?" Tom was angry.

"You better watch out, then." The driver studied Tom a moment. "You new around here? I haven't seen you before."

"We work for the Carlsons," Hallie spoke up.

"Squatters?"

She flinched. "Farmworkers."

"Taking jobs from local folks."

"Leave them alone, Harold," the second boy said. "They can't help it. They're just trying to make it, like everybody else."

"Yeah," Harold said. "Times are hard. Still, jobs ought to go to the people who live here."

"I have a stick." Benny came up to the car.

"It's bigger than you are," Harold laughed. He stared at Benny. "What's wrong with him?"

"Nothing," Hallie and Tom said together.

"Look at him, Dan. You ever see somebody that stupid-looking."

"Don't say 'stupid,'" Benny said.

"Don't tell me what to say."

"Oh, come on, Harold. He's just a kid. Leave him alone," Dan said.

"Yeah," Harold agreed. "Let's go." He gave Tom a curt nod and gunned the engine, then drove off, leaving a cloud of dust behind them.

"They're jerks, but that's a pretty nice car," Hallie said.

"It's an Essex Terraplane Deluxe Eight. I saw one like it in Oklahoma City. It costs more money than we'll make in a year—in ten years."

"I don't like him. He could have hit Benny."

"I guess it really wasn't his fault. We have to watch Benny when we're on the road."

Hallie nodded. They had to watch Benny wherever he was.

⌒

One evening a couple of weeks later, a black car stopped on the road near where the Turners were camped. Hallie felt uneasy and wondered if the car meant trouble. Then the back door opened. Tessie jumped out. "Hi, Benny," she called.

"Hi, Tessie. We have a fire. Be careful." He pointed to the coals in the fire circle, which was made of rocks.

"I'm careful."

The front doors of the car opened, and Mr. and Mrs. Carlson got out. Hallie had taken Benny to the Carlson place several times. Once she had helped Mrs. Carlson bottle tomatoes. Mrs. Carlson had given her four quarts of them. So they were eating red soup again. It wasn't so bad now, though, because Mrs. Carlson also sent them home with cake and a loaf of bread. She said the bread would get moldy in the heat if they didn't eat it.

Now Mr. Carlson said, "We have something to tell you."

Hallie glanced at Tom. He was staring at Mr. Carlson. She thought her brother was thinking the same thing she was: What if the Carlsons were there to tell them they didn't need the Turners anymore? Maybe Mr. Carlson would say it was time for them to move on. Hallie dug her toe into the dirt. She turned to see what Benny and Tessie were doing. Benny was showing his friend his boat and warning her to be careful of the water in the creek that ran by the camp.

Mrs. Carlson glanced at Tessie and Benny, too. Then she said, "I brought you something." She handed Hallie a glass jar. "Plum jam. My neighbor gave it to me, but we don't care for it. I hope you like it better than we do."

Hallie thanked her. She knew the Carlsons wouldn't drive down to the camp just to deliver a jar of jam, however.

Mr. Carlson cleared his throat, and Hallie tensed. Tom was chewing on his lip, which he did when he was nervous.

"The thing is, nobody's using it, so you might as well."

Hallie didn't understand. Was that his way of telling them they were no longer wanted?

"Sir?" Tom asked.

"You don't have to, of course. I'll understand if you say no."

Tom frowned. "What's that?"

"The old hired man's cabin. I was thinking it ought to be tore down and the land planted, but that don't make sense now, what with the prices I'm getting for crops. I'll get rid of it when things are better. Nobody's been there for a long time. It might not even be livable. You can move in there if you want to. Hot as it is now, it still won't be long before winter. If you're thinking of staying on for a time, you might as well take a look at it."

"Of course, you might not want to stay in Kansas more than another month or two. We understand that, too," Mrs. Carlson said. "Sometimes I wish myself I was in California."

Hallie wasn't sure she had heard right. "The cabin?" she asked.

"Oh, I told Mr. Carlson we might be insulting you by offering it. It's awful worn down. For all I know, it's got raccoons living in it. The place will take a powerful lot of cleaning, but you don't seem to mind cleaning," she said. "We worry about you living in a tent come winter—especially Benny."

"You're offering us the cabin?" Tom asked. He and Hallie looked at each other. They couldn't believe it.

"We can call it a loan," Mr. Carlson said. "Like I say, I was fixing on tearing it down one of these days on account of I can't afford a full-time hired man. Until prices pick up, I'll leave it alone. Last time I looked, it wasn't too bad. There's a glass window. I boarded it up so's nobody would break it."

"We saw the cabin was there. We sure do thank you, Mr. Carlson," Tom said, holding out his hand. The two shook.

"Don't thank him till you've seen it," Mrs. Carlson told him. "We can take a look at it now." She called Tessie, who held Benny's hand as the group walked through the woods to the cabin.

Mr. Carlson had brought along a crowbar. He and Tom pried the boards off the door and the window. The glass in the window was cracked, but it wasn't broken out. Tom and Mr. Carlson went inside first. Mr. Carlson came out looking relieved. "I was afraid maybe squat—that is, hobos might have got inside and tore it up, but it looks all right."

Hallie pushed past her brother and looked at the interior. There was an iron bedstead with rusted springs, a lopsided bureau missing two legs, and a broken chair. At one end was a stone fireplace. Hallie thought how nice it would be to use the fireplace instead of a campfire for cooking. "We'll have to check and make sure the stack's tight before you use it," Mr. Carlson said. "Wouldn't want to fill up the room with smoke."

"It's a house," Benny said.

"Now you can live inside," Tessie told him.

"Okay."

Mrs. Carlson inspected the place, then told Hallie, "Like I said, it needs cleaning. Some boards need tacking up. The floor's still good. I think I've got some old curtains. They're faded, but they'll do till you get better. And we have an extra kerosene lamp. Tom can haul out that old bed and springs if you don't want them."

"Oh, no. I want them. I've never slept in a bed before."

Mrs. Carlson looked surprised but said nothing. She and Hallie inspected the cabin. Hallie made a note of what had to be done. "I'll start cleaning in the morning," Hallie said.

"I'll come down later with a few things," Mrs. Carlson told her. "You'll need a broom and soap and cleaning rags."

The Carlsons went back to their car. Tom and Hallie walked beside them.

"We sure do thank you," Tom said.

Benny and Tessie played tag in the warm dusk, and the

others stood and talked for a moment, enjoying the breeze. After a time, they heard a car coming down the road. Hallie turned to see Harold driving the Terraplane.

Harold slowed when he saw them and yelled, "Evening, Mr. and Mrs. Carlson!" He ignored Tom and Hallie.

"That's Harold Morton. Where do you suppose he got that fancy car?" Mrs. Carlson asked.

"From his daddy. Mr. Morton spoils Harold as bad as sour milk," Mr. Carlson replied. Then he turned to Tom. "He thinks too high of himself. I advise you to stay clear of him."

"We met him already," Hallie said.

"I'm sorry about that."

The Carlsons left then. Tom and Hallie watched them drive away. "Mr. and Mrs. Carlson sure are nice folks, but I don't like that fellow Harold," Tom said.

"Me neither," Hallie replied. "Do you think he'll cause us trouble?"

Tom shrugged. "Probably not. I bet he thinks we're not worth it."

Hallie wasn't so sure. Since they had left Oklahoma, they had met a few nice people, like the Carlsons and the woman who'd given them the buttermilk. They'd met mean ones, too. She wondered how other people in the area would treat them. For a moment, she felt prickly with the worry of it. Then she turned her thoughts to the cabin. It was rickety, but it was better than the tent. For the first time since they left Cookietown, they would sleep under a roof.

⁓

"Let's get to work," Mrs. Carlson said when she arrived early the next morning at the Turners' campsite. Tessie had come, too. They brought a broom, a mop, two pails, soap, and ammonia, along with other cleaning supplies. Hallie started to take them from her, but Mrs. Carlson said, "Not on your life. You don't think I'm going to leave you with that filthy place to clean by yourself, do you? This is a job for the two of us."

Hallie looked at her in surprise, then grinned. "I can't pay you twenty-five cents."

Mrs. Carlson laughed. "It's what neighbors do. Now let's get started. I told Mr. Carlson he and Tom would find their dinner in the refrigerator." This was one of Tom's days to work for Mr. Carlson. "I brought ours along with me." She led the way to the cabin, with Hallie, Benny, and Tessie following behind.

"I can sweep," Tessie said, swiping the broom across the leaves.

"Me too," Benny said.

Inside the cabin, Mrs. Carlson put her hands on her hips. "Worse than I thought in the dark last night," she said. "Let's clear it out."

The four of them dragged boxes of moldy clothes, broken dishes, old newspapers, and pots with rusted-out bottoms to the campsite's fireplace circle. "I'll tackle the window," Mrs. Carlson said. The window was covered with so much grime that the daylight couldn't come through. When the window was clean, the sun shone into the cabin.

"I'll clean the burnt sticks and ashes out of the fireplace and scrub it," Hallie told her.

"We're sweeping," Tessie said. She and Benny took turns with the broom until they both were covered with dust. While Hallie stood on the bedsprings to wipe the dirt and cobwebs from the ceiling, Mrs. Carlson scrubbed the walls. Then they washed the bureau and propped it up on blocks of wood.

They finished the cleaning by noon, then sat by the stream to eat the dinner Mrs. Carlson had brought. "I surely do thank you," Hallie said.

"Oh, we're not through yet. Now that we've done the dirty work, we have the fun part. We'll make up beds and unpack your boxes and put things away." So the four of them dismantled the camp and carried everything but the tent to the cabin. They spread one of the mattresses on the springs and put the other on the floor. "Who gets the bed?" Mrs. Carlson asked.

"I do," Benny replied.

"I guess we'll take turns, Benny," Hallie said.

"Okay."

They spread the quilts on top of the mattresses, then started putting the Turners' belongings away. They lined the bureau drawers with newspaper and placed the clothes in the drawers. Then they arranged the tin dishes and pots on top of the bureau. Finally, Mrs. Carlson took out a pair of curtains she had brought and nailed them to the window. She stood back and looked at the room and nodded. "It's nothing fancy, but it's better than it was. And like the man says, it'll keep the rain out."

"We're not done," Hallie told her. She went to the last box and took out a quilt. It was white with tiny blue squares in a crisscross design.

"An Irish Chain," Mrs. Carlson murmured. "Oh my. It's as fine a quilt as I ever saw. Did you make it?"

Hallie shook her head. "Mommy did. It was her prize quilt. We gave away most of her other quilts when we left Oklahoma, but I couldn't leave this one." The two of them nailed the quilt to the wall over the bed.

Mrs. Carlson pinched a corner of the quilt between her fingers. "I never saw such fine stitches."

"Mommy was the best quilter in the county. Everybody said so," Hallie told her.

"This would win a prize all right. Did she teach you?"

"I never cared much for quilting, but I'm sorry now I didn't learn."

Mrs. Carlson thought that over. "I could teach you. It's not hard. I could show you next time you bring Benny to play. I'd rather quilt than eat pie."

"I'd like that," Hallie said, "although I'd rather eat pie than quilt."

Happy Days

*B*y fall, the Turners had been living on the Carlson farm for several weeks, and it looked as if they might stay on in the cabin for a time. One day, Hallie walked into town with Benny. They had made the mile walk before to go to the mercantile or to meet Tom. He worked two days a week now at the garage and filling station.

Tom hadn't expected to get the job. After all, there were local boys who wanted to work at the garage, and he was an outsider. The day he applied, however, Mr. Ulman, who owned the garage, had the hood up on a car. He was peering inside and shook his head when Tom walked in. "I'll hire you if you can tell me what's wrong with this engine," he said.

He'd meant it as a joke. He hadn't really expected Tom to figure out the problem. To Mr. Ulman's surprise, Tom had ducked his head under the hood and tinkered a moment. Then he pointed to what was wrong. He worked on the engine a few minutes and fixed it.

"I been studying on that car for two days and ain't figured it out, and you did it in five minutes," Mr. Ulman said. "By Jove, boy, if you want that job, it's yours. I'll give you work two days a week and pay you a dollar and a quarter."

"Mr. Carlson pays me a dollar a day," Tom said, holding his breath for fear Mr. Ulman would think he was greedy.

"That's a dollar and twenty-five *a day*. You can work on your own automobile here when we're not busy."

Tom had gulped. That was better pay than farmwork. Besides, he'd rather fix motors than plow and weed. He grinned at Mr. Ulman. "Yes, sir. Thank you, sir," he said.

Now Tom had been employed at the garage for a month. Mr. Ulman had told him he was a worker. That was high praise.

This day Hallie wasn't going to town to see Tom. She had washed Benny in the creek, soaped his hair, too, and dressed him in clean clothes. He had put on his new shoes, the ones Tom had bought him. With money coming in, the Turners had replaced their worn-out clothing and bought a few things for the cabin. They were eating better, too.

"Where are we going, Hallie?" Benny asked.

"To the school."

"I want to go to school."

"Do you remember your letters?"

" 'A' is for 'apple,' " he said.

"What else?"

" 'B' for 'baby.' "

"What's next?"

" 'D' is 'dog.' "

"You forgot 'C.' "

" 'Cat.' "

"And 'E'?"

"I can't remember."

" 'Elephant.' "

"I can't say 'l-font.' "

"That's good enough." She took Benny's hand and led him into the school, which was near the center of town. They found the principal's office.

A woman was sitting at a desk. She looked up and smiled. "How can I help you?"

Hallie was nervous. All the way into town, she had practiced in her mind what she would say. Now, however, the words escaped her.

"Yes?" the woman said, a questioning look on her face.

"Are you in charge?" Hallie asked. She stood up as straight as she could so that she would look older and more confident.

The woman nodded. "Yes. I am the principal."

"I'm Hallie. That is, I'm Hazel Rose Turner. I want to sign up for eighth grade."

The principal wrote down Hallie's name on a list of students. "School will be starting soon. Your teacher will be Mrs. Powell. Her room is down the hall, the last door on the left. You're all set."

Hallie sighed in relief. *Maybe registering for school is easier than I thought.* She said, "This is my brother Benny. He needs to go to school, too. First grade. He's six."

"Hi, I'm Benny," Benny said.

When Hallie glanced at her brother, she saw with horror that Benny was sitting on the floor, taking off his shoes.

"Benny!" she said.

Benny looked up and smiled. "I have shoes."

Hallie turned back to the principal and explained, "They're new. They hurt his feet." When the woman didn't reply, Hallie said anxiously, "Benny already knows his letters. What's 'A' for, Benny?"

"'Baby,'" Benny replied.

"You know it's for 'apple.' What's 'C'?"

Benny looked confused. "I don't know, Hallie."

"It's 'cat,' Benny."

"I saw Bob," Benny told the principal.

The woman shifted in her chair. "Do you live around here?"

"We live on the Carlson place," Hallie told her.

"Oh yes, I've heard about you. In the hired man's cabin, isn't it?"

"We're not squatters. They told us we could live there."

"You're the children who live by themselves, aren't you?"

"My brother Tom's sixteen."

"I see."

"Benny's six. He wants to go to first grade."

The woman sighed and said not unkindly, "I'm afraid we

can't allow that."

"But he has to," Hallie said. "He wants to learn. How can he learn to read if he doesn't go to school?" Then she said something that had been weighing on her mind. "I have it all planned out. I want to finish the eighth grade. I can't do that if Benny's not in school, too. You see, there's nobody to take care of him." She knew she sounded desperate, but she couldn't help it.

"I'm sorry, but we can't allow children such as your brother here in the school. He will be disruptive. We have to think of the other pupils. Besides, you people will be moving on soon."

Hallie flinched at the words "you people." The woman might as well have said outright, "You squatters."

"We're not moving on. We're staying."

The principal stood. "As I said, I am sorry about your brother, but we have rules. I must abide by them. You'll have to find something suitable for the boy."

"He's not 'the boy.' His name is Benny," Hallie flared.

"Good luck to you." The principal glanced down at her desk and moved some papers around. Hallie knew she had been dismissed.

"Come on, Benny. We know when we're not good enough."

"I didn't say that—"

Hallie didn't reply. She picked up Benny's shoes. She took his hand and led him out of the room. There wouldn't be any school for Benny. There wouldn't be any school for her, either. She'd counted on finishing the eighth grade, but that wasn't going to happen. She should have told the principal to take her name off the list.

"I go to school, Hallie?" Benny said as they went down the steps.

"Not this year, Benny."

"Why?"

She wanted to reply that the school was unfair, that it didn't care about children who were different. Benny wouldn't understand why he wasn't allowed to attend school. He didn't know some children learned slower than others. He didn't know he was not like the other students. Instead, Hallie said, "No room."

"I want to."

"I want you to, too, but I can't do anything about it."

"Okay," Benny said. " 'G' for 'goat.' "

"I'm so sorry, but I'm not surprised," Mrs. Carlson said when Hallie told her what had happened at the school. The two sat in the shade of a trumpet vine on the Carlsons' porch with their quilt scraps. Mrs. Carlson was showing Hallie how to make a nine-patch square. It was made up of nine two-inch squares stitched together in rows of three. Hallie had cut the pieces a little larger than two inches to allow for seams. When the pieces were sewn together, they would make a six-inch square block. Hallie used a piece of cardboard as a pattern. "Try this green material. It will be pretty with your yellow," Mrs. Carlson said, reaching into her ragbag.

She continued. "I should have warned you. I tried to enroll Tessie last year. The school wouldn't take her. Mr. Carlson even talked to members of the school board. They wouldn't budge. Benny knows his letters, so I thought maybe he'd be accepted."

Hallie shook her head.

Mrs. Carlson stitched on her own quilt pieces for a moment, thinking. She glanced over at Hallie's sewing and told her to make the seams larger so that the squares wouldn't pull out. Then she asked, "Did you sign up for school yourself?"

"Yes, but I don't know why. I won't be able to go."

"Because of Benny?"

Hallie nodded. "Tom and I talked about it. He could watch Benny on the days he doesn't work. But he spends two days at the garage, and then he'll be helping Mr. Carlson with the harvest." She realized what she'd said and added quickly, "I mean we're really grateful he has the work. We couldn't make it if he didn't. We're awful glad Mr. Carlson gave him the job." She feared Mrs. Carlson might repeat what she'd said to her husband, and he would cut back on Tom's days. That would be disastrous.

"Could you get your schoolwork done if you go just a couple of days a week? Maybe one of your schoolmates would help you." Mrs. Carlson stared at Hallie, whose eyes were on her sewing. "Have you met any other girls your age here?"

Hallie didn't look up but shook her head.

"Oh, my dear, I am so sorry." Mrs. Carlson put down her piecing and put her hand on Hallie's arm. "You are just a young girl and an orphan. Yet you have the responsibilities of a woman. It must be so hard. You don't have any friends, do you?"

"I have you."

Mrs. Carlson put her hand to her eye and wiped away a tear. "Life is difficult for all of us but especially for you."

"There's Tom. And Benny."

"Do you ever resent your little brother?"

Hallie looked up. "No."

"I shouldn't say this, but I will tell you that I did at first, with Tessie. But now I can't imagine my life without her. She is such a dear little girl. I feel blessed. I wouldn't have her any other way." She glanced up at Benny and Tessie, who were playing with Tessie's Lincoln Logs. They were trying to build a house with them. They laughed when the walls fell down.

Tessie began chewing on one of the logs. Mrs. Carlson got up to take it away from her, but Benny said, "Don't eat that. It's dirty." Tessie put it down.

"I believe she's learned something from him in the short time she's known him," Mrs. Carlson said. "Her speech has improved."

The children had put aside the logs and were now scratching in the dirt with sticks. "I'm glad Benny has a friend," Hallie said. "He would be sad if he didn't."

The two sat in the porch shade stitching for a long time. Every now and then, Mrs. Carlson examined Hallie's work and made suggestions. "I have a feed sack with just the right flowers to go with the yellow and green. Don't let me forget it," Mrs. Carlson said. Hallie knew that manufacturers of bulk items such as chicken feed packaged the contents in fabric bags with colorful designs on them. Women picked the designs they liked best and then cut up the bags after they were empty. They made dresses and shirts and even underwear from them. They used the scraps for quilts. Hallie's two dresses, in fact, had been made from feed sacks back in Oklahoma. Hallie had seen Mrs. Carlson's stash of feed sacks with flowers and animals and Persian pickles on them.

Mrs. Carlson put her sewing aside, saying she was going to fetch iced tea for the two of them. Hallie hadn't had iced tea for a long time. She hadn't had ice for a long time, either.

Mrs. Carlson called Tessie and Benny to her. "Would you like iced tea?" she asked.

"Yay!" Tessie said.

Benny looked at Hallie. He'd never had the drink. "It's cold tea. You'll like it," Hallie told him.

"Okay."

"Okay. Thank you," Hallie told him.

"Okay."

Tessie had begun scratching in the dirt of the flower bed with her stick, and Mrs. Carlson was about to tell the girl to dig elsewhere, when she narrowed her eyes. "What's that you're drawing, Tessie?" she asked.

" 'A' for 'apple,' " Tessie said proudly.

Mrs. Carlson leaned over and studied the ground. She looked up at Hallie. "That does indeed look like an 'A.' " She turned to Tessie. "Where did you learn that?"

" 'A' for apple,' " Tessie said again. " 'C' for 'cat.' Benny told me."

"Does Benny know all the alphabet?" Mrs. Carlson asked Hallie.

"Some of it."

"I showed Tessie," Benny said.

Mrs. Carlson sat down on the porch steps. "For the past year, I've tried to teach Tessie her letters, but she just won't learn them. Do you think Benny actually taught them to her?"

Hallie shrugged. "Maybe. I think they learn from each

other. The other day he told me that ice is frozen water."

"Tessie must have taught him that. I explained it to her after a piece of ice melted." Mrs. Carlson looked up at Hallie. "It seems like they teach each other. I wonder if they learn better if they're together."

Mrs. Carlson stood up and went into the house then. In a few moments, she returned with a tray carrying four glasses of iced tea. She called Tessie and Benny and gave them the tea. They drank it quickly. Tessie put a piece of ice down Benny's shirt. The two of them laughed and ran off. Mrs. Carlson sat down and picked up her sewing, but she didn't take a stitch. "Something occurred to me just now," she said.

Hallie looked at a seam she had made. Her stitches were big and sloppy. She took them out, saving the thread to be reused.

"If Tessie and Benny learn better together, why don't we set up our own school with just the two of them?" Mrs. Carlson asked.

Hallie was threading her needle and stopped with the end of the thread in her mouth.

"I will take them two days a week. Perhaps you could take them from time to time when you're free," Mrs. Carlson continued. "That way, you will have two more days to attend school. Do you think that might work?"

Hallie removed the thread from her mouth and looked up at Mrs. Carlson. Her throat felt tight. All she could do was nod and mutter, "I think so."

Hallie and Benny sang "Happy Days" as they walked along the dirt road back to the cabin. Benny was barefoot. Hallie was saving his shoes for winter. Every now and then, he curled his toes and flicked the road dust out in front of him. He kicked a rock and said, "Ouch!" when the rock didn't move. "Happy days," he said, and Hallie thought he was right. Thanks to the Carlsons, there were happy days to look forward to. Hallie could start eighth grade again, and Benny and Tessie would have their own lessons.

"You're going to go to school, Benny," Hallie told him.

"Okay."

"It's a very special school, and only you and Tessie can attend."

"What's attend?"

"It means you and Tessie are the only ones in the whole school."

Benny looked confused. "That school?"

"No, it's a school at Tessie's house, and sometimes Tessie will come to our place."

"Tessie's my friend. I taught her 'A,' 'B,' 'C,' 'E,' 'A' . . ." He listed a dozen letters of the alphabet. Then he asked, "Are you coming to my school, Hallie?"

"I can't. It's only for you and Tessie."

"Too bad." He grinned up at his sister. She took his hand, thinking how well things had turned out. Tom had a job, they had a place to live, and now both Hallie and Benny could attend school. Of course, it might not be for long. Maybe the depression would get worse, and there wouldn't be any work at all. Or the Carlsons' harvest might be a dud. The garage could close. They might have to go on to California after all. There was plenty for her to worry about. But for now, she was happier than she had been since leaving Oklahoma. Both she and Benny were going to school.

She took Benny's hand when she heard a fast automobile behind them. She had to be sure Benny didn't dash out in front of the car. Now she looked to see who was coming. She recognized Harold's Terraplane. "Oh darn," she muttered to herself. She thought he would go on by, but instead, he pulled over to her side of the road. Dan sat in the car beside him. Both of them were smoking cigarettes. Hallie wondered why anybody would waste money on ready-made cigarettes. The two boys must indeed be rich.

"You still squatting around here?" Harold asked.

"We're not squatters."

"So you say. What do you say, Dan?"

Dan looked uncomfortable and shrugged. "Come on. Let's go."

"I got no place to go. Do you?"

"Leave her alone, Harold."

"Your brother took my job," Harold said.

"You were going to work for Mr. Carlson?" Hallie asked. She couldn't imagine Harold getting his nice clothes dirty doing farm chores.

"Funny, isn't she?" Harold asked Dan. He turned to Hallie. "Your brother took my job at the garage. I was talking to Mr. Ulman about working there when your brother came along. He got hired instead of me. I say hire local boys instead of Okies."

"Oh, come on, Harold. How long do you think you'd last pumping gas all day?" Dan asked. "You didn't even want that job."

"Maybe I did. It was as good as mine until squatter boy there came along."

Benny had been staring at the car. He said, "Hi, I'm Benny."

"It's that stupid kid," Harold said.

"Don't say 'stupid,' " Benny told him.

"Oh, that's right. How about 'dummy,' then?"

Benny looked at Hallie. "He said a bad word."

Dan tapped Harold's arm with his fist. "Let up on them."

"Yeah, sorry, kid. Your brother isn't your fault."

Hallie remembered what Mr. Carlson had said about Harold. She didn't want to cause trouble for Tom. "My brother didn't know that was your job. He wouldn't take work away from anyone."

"Harold wouldn't have gotten that job anyway. He knows as much about fixing cars as a cat does about Christmas." Dan leaned over his friend and smiled at Hallie. She thought he was nicer than Harold.

"What do you know?" Harold said.

"The way you drive this car, who'd hire you for a mechanic? Look at that taillight. You dinged that up pretty bad."

Hallie looked at the back of the car and saw that a taillight was broken. There was a long scratch on the driver's-side door, too.

"Shut up or you can walk," Harold told Dan.

"Don't say 'shut up,'" Benny said.

"Tell that kid to watch his mouth," Harold told Hallie. He put in the clutch, shifted into first gear, and shot off, grinding the gears.

Hallie stared after him.

Benny said, "Bad boy."

chapter five

School Days

*H*allie and Benny started school on the same day. Tom had bought Benny a red tablet with the picture of an Indian chief on the cover and a yellow pencil. Tom had sharpened the pencil with his pocketknife. The day was warm. Benny could have gone barefoot, but he wanted to wear his new shoes. Tom and Hallie together walked him to the Carlson house. Mrs. Carlson had set pillows on two chairs at the dining room table so the children could sit up high enough to write. A cowbell sat on the table. Mrs. Carlson explained that she would ring the bell when school started and when it was time for recess.

"Recess means it's time to play," Hallie whispered.

Benny nodded.

Hallie hugged her brother, and Tom squeezed the little boy's shoulder. "You be good, Ben. No talking back to the teacher," he said.

"I'm good," Benny told him.

Hallie could see that her older brother was as moved as she was that Benny was going to "school." He worried about Benny, too. Tom was the head of the family now. It wasn't easy for him having to care for a brother and sister. He could have disappeared the way Daddy did. Hallie knew that Tom wouldn't do that. He wouldn't desert them any more than she would.

At first, Hallie had blamed Daddy for leaving them. Since she'd been on the road, however, she'd come to understand why Daddy had never come back home. There hadn't been any work for him. He probably had thought he was a failure and couldn't face Mommy and the rest of the family. He was ashamed that he couldn't provide for them. It had been easier just to drift away than to come home and look at his family's disappointed faces. He'd feel he'd let them down. During the months she and Tom and Benny had been traveling,

Hallie had seen too many men like Daddy. They wandered the roads as if they were lost. Their shoulders were slumped. There was no hope in their faces. Like them, Daddy had given up. But Tom was made of sterner stuff. Hallie would always be able to count on him.

"That was nice of you to buy Benny the tablet," Hallie said. "And the shoes."

"I should have bought shoes for you, too."

"I already have shoes." Hallie had found a piece of cardboard on the road the day before. She'd taken it home and made inserts to fit inside her shoes. They would cover the holes in the soles. She'd saved the rest of the cardboard because the insets wouldn't last forever.

"I'm glad you figured out a way to go to school, Hallie," he said. "That's a weight off my mind."

Hallie didn't say anything. It would be hard, attending school only a few days a week. Still, she'd make it work. She knew that her graduating from eighth grade was as important to Tom as it was to her. Tom hadn't let her down. She wouldn't let him down, either.

That was going to be hard, because by the dinner break on the first day of the school year, Hallie was beginning to wonder if she had made a mistake. She had loved school in Oklahoma. Everyone there was her friend. She'd played hopscotch and jumped rope with the other girls. They'd shared secrets and traded food from their dinner sacks and walked to and from the school together. Except for Harold and Dan, she hadn't met any other students until that first day. By noon, she didn't like any of them.

Hallie wore a new dress that Mrs. Carlson had made for her from two feed sacks. Hallie had chosen the material. The dress was pink with rosebuds sprinkled over it. It had a sash and a white collar, and there was rickrack down the front. It was the prettiest dress Hallie had ever worn. She'd rubbed her shoes with bacon grease until they shone. She'd braided her hair three times until she was satisfied. She didn't have a mirror, so she couldn't see her appearance. Still, she knew she looked her best. Tom said she'd never looked better. Even Benny grinned at her and said, "Pretty."

She made a bean sandwich for herself and put it into a sugar sack to carry to school. Then just before they left the cabin, Tom took out a second tablet exactly like Benny's. He gave it to Hallie. "The smartest girl in the class has to have something to write on," he said.

Hallie arrived a few minutes before the bell rang. She stood in the schoolyard staring at the other students. Hallie watched the youngest children play tag, wishing Benny could have been among them. Then she studied the older students. They were the ones who would be in her grade. A few of them glanced at her, but they turned away, ignoring her. The bell rang, and the students, including Hallie, went inside the school. But Hallie got confused and went the wrong way to her classroom. She had to backtrack and ended up being the last one in the room. All the seats were taken except for those in the very front row. Since the door was in the back, she had to walk past everyone to sit down. She felt the others staring at her, which made her nervous. She dropped her tablet, and someone snickered. She didn't feel so smart then.

The teacher welcomed the students and introduced herself as Mrs. Powell. She said there were several who had not been in school last year. She asked them to introduce themselves, too.

"I'm Cathy. We moved here from Topeka to live on my grandparents' farm," one girl announced.

"My name's Dorothy. I'm living with Wilma. She's my cousin."

Hallie turned to stare at her. Wilma would be the girl next to Dorothy, wearing a store-bought dress and patent leather shoes. The other girls had been gathered around her in the playground. She must be the most popular girl in school. Hallie remembered when *she* had been the most popular one at the school in Oklahoma.

A new boy introduced himself. Then the teacher looked at Hallie. "I believe you're new here, too, aren't you?" She looked down at a list of student names. "Hazel, is it?"

"Hallie. I'm Hallie Turner."

"And are you living with your family?"

"I live on the Carlson place with my brothers," she said.

"Squatters," someone whispered. "That isn't their home."

Hallie looked around and glared. But she wasn't sure who had spoken. The teacher rapped her desk with a ruler and said, "Quiet."

Hallie slunk down in her seat. She was silent during most of the morning, but when the teacher pulled down a map hanging above the blackboard and began a lesson in geography, Hallie sat up straight. She never knew why the subject fascinated her. She loved to dream about far-off places and the people who lived there. Her teacher in Oklahoma had come from England, and some of the settlers around Cookietown had emigrated from Russia and Poland. Hallie had found their countries on the map. The teacher once loaned her an atlas, and Hallie had studied the different countries.

Now Mrs. Powell explained about continents. She asked if anyone knew how many there were. Hallie raised her hand. She glanced around and saw that she was the only one with her hand up. She quickly pulled it down but not before the teacher saw it. "How many, Hallie?" she asked.

"Seven."

"Can you name them?"

Hallie ducked her head. She didn't want to appear to show off. "I guess so."

"Then do it, please."

"North America, South America," she began. Her voice got softer as she named each one.

"Very good. Now does anyone know which continent Kansas is in?"

"Ask Miss Know-It-All," a girl said. Hallie thought the

voice might be Wilma's.

"Knowledge is something to be proud of," the teacher said. "Ignorance is to be pitied."

Hallie slunk farther down in her seat. She was grateful that Mrs. Powell gave the answer to the question instead of calling on her again.

⁓

As bad as class had been during the morning, Hallie was afraid the dinner break would be even worse. There wouldn't be any teacher to keep order. When the bell rang, she was slow in straightening her tablet and making sure her pencil was secure beside it. She picked up the sugar sack with her sandwich and went outside. She hoped she could find a place where she could eat by herself. It was clear she hadn't made any friends. She sat down on the grass. She grew nervous when a group of girls, Wilma at the center, sat down near her. One of the girls turned to Hallie and asked, "Are you really a squatter?"

"No," Hallie replied.

"Of course she is," Wilma said.

"No, I'm not!" Hallie told her.

"Yes, you are," Dorothy said. "What else do you call people who live on your land and don't work and don't pay rent?"

"Relatives," Hallie blurted out.

Wilma's mouth dropped open. Dorothy glared at Hallie. "What did you say that for?" Wilma asked.

The other girls covered their mouths to hide their giggles. The girl named Cathy laughed out loud and said, "That's a good one."

~

"I like school," Benny said. Since Tom had worked for Mr. Carlson that day, he brought Benny home with him. " 'Z' is for 'horse.' "

" 'H' is for 'horse,' " Hallie said.

"No, 'Z.' I saw the picture."

"The word's 'zebra,' " Tom explained. "Mrs. Carlson showed me a new alphabet book she bought for Tessie."

"What's a zebra?" Hallie had never heard of such an animal.

"A striped horse. So Benny got it right."

"What did you do at school?" Hallie asked her little brother.

"I can read."

"Already?"

Benny nodded. "I saw 'A' in a book. I can read 'A.' We had apple pie. 'A' for 'apple pie.'"

"What about 'B'?" Tom asked.

"Next time."

"Did you play?"

"Recess. We played recess."

"What about *your* school?" Tom asked Hallie. "Did you play recess, too?" He grinned.

Hallie didn't answer, and Tom asked, "Did you make any friends."

"No, but I might have made enemies. They all think we're squatters."

"Well, we aren't," Tom told her. "Did you tell them that?"

"I tried to."

"But?"

Hallie shrugged.

"You won't quit school, will you?" Tom asked.

"No." Hallie shook her head. "We're not quitters. Still,

it's hard when they think they're better than we are."

"They're not. Some of those people are as poor as us."

"I know," Hallie agreed. She remembered the children whose dinner sacks were as meager as hers. There were boys whose overalls were ragged, and girls with dresses too short and too tight. But they had lived in the area for a long time, so nobody called them squatters. She thought, too, about Wilma and Dorothy and two or three other girls. They were wearing new clothes and had cheese or peanut butter sandwiches on store-bought bread. And cookies or cake for dessert. They were the ones who looked down on her.

"Ignore the rich kids," Tom said. He seemed to know what she was thinking. "You can find other girls to be your friends."

"Tessie's your friend," Benny put in.

That made Hallie smile. "And you're my friend, too, Benny. You're my special friend." *Things could be a lot worse,* Hallie thought. At least she had her brothers.

⌒

Hallie and Tom were preparing dinner. Tom built a fire in the fireplace, while Hallie mixed up batter for flapjacks.

When the fire had burned down a little and the coals were hot, she set a cast-iron skillet on the coals and added grease from the tin can of bacon fat she had saved. Then she poured the pancake batter into the hot pan. "Cooking in a fireplace is better than cooking over a campfire, but I'd still give anything for a cook stove like we had back home. I burned the yeast bread I made yesterday."

"I have a surprise for you, then. I was going to wait until later, after it was set up, but I'll tell you now." Tom grinned. "Mrs. Carlson says we can have her old cook stove. She had it hauled to the barn after she got that fancy new one. She said she'd forgotten all about it or she would have offered it to us earlier. Mr. Carlson and I will set it up."

"Imagine! A cook stove just like home," Hallie said. "I can cook on it, and it will keep us warm in the winter." *Will we be here for the winter?* Hallie wondered.

Hallie stayed in the cabin the next day, because Tom was working at the garage. Since Mrs. Carlson had taught Tessie and Benny the day before, Benny was home, too. Hallie did her arithmetic homework and read a chapter in a book Mrs. Powell had assigned. The book was old. Some of the pages were missing. But at least the school provided the readers. She didn't have to buy one.

When she showed up for school on Wednesday, Wilma remarked, "Oh, I thought you'd quit."

Hallie was so mad that she stuck out her tongue at Wilma. Only later did she wonder if she'd been wrong. Maybe Wilma wasn't being nasty. Maybe she had just made an observation. Hallie didn't know for sure, but it didn't matter. No way would she apologize.

In class, Hallie was aware she was a day behind. Everyone had already turned in the arithmetic she had done at home and had even completed another assignment for Wednesday. The class was further ahead in the reader than she was, too. At the dinner break, Mrs. Powell asked her to stay behind.

"You were absent yesterday," Mrs. Powell said after the others had gone.

"Yes, ma'am."

"Do you want to tell me why?"

Hallie looked down at her shoes. There was a hole in the toe of her right shoe. She hadn't seen that before. "I have to look after my little brother."

"What about your mother?"

"She died." Hallie felt her eyes well up.

"And your father?"

Hallie shrugged. She didn't want to talk about her parents.

"I see. You said you live on the Carlson place. Do the Carlsons take care of you?"

"We take care of ourselves," Hallie said fiercely.

The teacher studied Hallie a moment. "And proud of it, I see." Then she asked, "How many days a week do you expect to be away from school?"

"One or two—three if my older brother's working." Hallie couldn't look at the teacher. Mrs. Powell was probably going to tell her she had to drop out. That would give her an excuse to leave school. Tom couldn't call her a quitter if Mrs. Powell wouldn't let her stay in school. She thought that over. Two days before she wasn't sure she wanted to finish eighth grade, but suddenly, she was angry. What right did that teacher have to tell her she couldn't attend? Mrs. Powell didn't know her at all. She had no reason to assume she couldn't keep up. "I can do the work, Mrs. Powell. Just you wait and see."

The teacher smiled at her. "I hoped you'd say that. So many migrant children are discouraged, but you have a spark in you. I saw that the first day of school. You let me know the days you'll be absent, and I'll be sure to tell you what you have to do to keep up. I believe everyone deserves an education." Mrs. Powell stood up to dismiss Hallie, then sat down again. "There's one other thing. Don't you ever let the others get away with calling you a squatter. You're no such thing. You're just as good as anybody else."

Hallie couldn't believe the teacher was being so nice. She wondered if she ought to stay in the schoolroom and eat her dinner with Mrs. Powell. The teacher picked up her dinner pail, however, and headed for the door. Hallie searched for her own sack, but it wasn't where she had put it. She looked inside her desk, then got down on her knees and looked under the desk. The sack was gone. Somebody had stolen it.

chapter six

Jimmy

*H*allie looked around the schoolyard. The other children were sitting in groups, eating their dinners. Wilma glanced up at Hallie, but quickly looked away. Hallie figured she was not welcome to join Wilma and her friends. For a moment, she wondered if Wilma had taken her dinner. Wilma wouldn't have wanted to eat Hallie's bean sandwich, but she might have swiped it just to be mean. Still, Hallie didn't know if Wilma was that spiteful. She looked around to see who else might have stolen her dinner. Someone must have taken it at recess. She tried to remember if any of the students had lagged behind when the others went outside.

She hadn't paid attention and couldn't think of anyone.

Then Hallie spotted Jimmy Watson. He was one of the boys who had called her a squatter that first day. Mrs. Powell already had broken up a fight between Jimmy and another boy. Hallie wondered if he was a bully. The other students seemed afraid of him.

Jimmy held a sugar sack in one hand and a sandwich in the other. The sack was the size of the one Hallie had brought to school, but then all sugar sacks looked alike. Most sandwiches looked alike, too.

Jimmy smirked at her. Hallie was pretty sure then that he'd taken her dinner. She wanted to go over and demand he give it back. But she didn't have any proof. What if she was wrong? That would be even more embarrassing. *Would I ever make friends after that?* she asked herself. So she sat on the steps by herself, glaring at anybody who came close.

That evening, she told Tom about the boy. She wondered if she should have confronted Jimmy after all. "Maybe I should have said something to him," she said.

"You could have," Tom responded. "But then he'd say that was his dinner. How would you prove it wasn't? You'd just be accused of causing trouble. You made the right decision."

"Well, he won't steal my dinner again," Hallie said.

"You'll keep an eye on it, then?"

"I'll do better than that." The next morning, Hallie made her sandwich. Then she took out another sugar sack. She didn't put her sandwich into the sack yet. Instead, she picked up her pencil and wrote "Hallie" in big black letters. "Now I'll know if anybody steals my dinner," she said.

When she settled into her desk at school, she placed her dinner sack on top of her tablet. Anybody could see her name written on it. She turned around and grinned at Jimmy, then pointed to the sack.

Jimmy shrugged, as if he didn't know what she was talking about.

Nobody stole Hallie's dinner after that. Still, Jimmy seemed to make a point of being mean to her. He stepped on her foot. He bumped her against the wall as they were leaving the room. He brushed by her desk and knocked her tablet onto the floor. "Hey!" Hallie said.

"Oops, sorry," he replied, but he wasn't sorry. He stepped

on the tablet before he picked it up, leaving a shoe print on the cover.

Hallie couldn't get the mark off, and she fumed. "You jerk," she muttered.

"Hey, it was an accident."

Hallie knew it wasn't. "What did I ever do to you?" she demanded.

"You're a squatter."

One day, a week later, Hallie heard a grade-school boy on the playground complain that his dinner had disappeared. Hallie had noticed the boy before because he looked rich. He wore store-bought clothes and usually had cake or cookies in his sack. She didn't know him, but still, she didn't like the idea of anybody stealing dinners.

"Come with me. Maybe I know who has it," she said. She took the boy's hand and led him over to where Jimmy sat. Jimmy was just removing food from a sack.

"That's my dinner!" the boy said.

"No, it ain't. I brung it from home," Jimmy said.

"It's got my birthday cake. See right there," the boy told Hallie. "Yesterday was my birthday."

"It was my birthday, too," Jimmy replied.

"Give it back to him," Hallie said. She started to raise her voice so that everybody knew Jimmy was a thief. Exposing him would be a good way to get back at him. But something told her not to do that. Maybe she ought to give Jimmy a chance to admit he was wrong.

"Mind your own business," Jimmy said.

"You going to make me?" Hallie asked.

"Aw, shut up. Take the dinner. Maybe I made a mistake." He dumped the cake into the bag and held it out to the boy. "Who wants cake anyway?"

The boy took the sack and grinned at Hallie, then raced off.

"It's pretty low to steal from a little kid," Hallie told Jimmy.

She turned away and went to the steps to eat by herself. A few minutes later, Cathy, the new girl who lived on her grandparents' farm, came over and sat beside Hallie. "Standing up for that little boy was a nice thing to do," she told Hallie.

Hallie shrugged. "I think Jimmy took my dinner once. That's wrong."

"He didn't do it for himself."

"What do you mean?" Hallie had removed her bean sandwich and saw to her surprise that Cathy was eating the same thing.

"Didn't you see that little kid beside him? That's Jimmy's brother. Jimmy steals food sometimes so that his brother can eat."

"Don't they bring their own dinners?"

"Not very often. When they do, it's just bacon grease spread on moldy bread. I saw it once. They get the bread from the grocery store after it's gone bad."

"That's icky," Hallie said. Even if she was hungry, she didn't think she would eat bread with mold on it. "How do you know?"

"They live on the farm next to us. Jimmy's dad drinks, and his mother is sick. They don't have anything. His father's mean. He beats up Jimmy and his brother. I know because Dad heard the boys hollering. He went over to find out if something was wrong. He saw Jimmy trying to protect his brother. Dad says Mr. Watson was yelling at Jimmy that he ought to quit school so he could help with the farm."

"Maybe that's where Jimmy gets his meanness."

Cathy shrugged. "Maybe he's that way to cover up that

he's scared all the time."

"Really?" Hallie had to think about that for a minute.

"That's what my mom says anyway."

"Do they go hungry?"

"I don't know, but it wouldn't surprise me. I think that's why he steals dinners. I've noticed that when they eat, Jimmy makes his brother take most of the food. Jimmy always says he isn't hungry."

The bell rang then, and the two girls picked up their sugar sacks. "I'm glad you told me," Hallie said.

"Don't say anything to anybody else. Jimmy would be embarrassed." Cathy smiled. "Besides, I wouldn't want him to get mad at *me*."

"I won't." Hallie paused. "Thanks for eating dinner with me."

Cathy nodded. "Let's do it tomorrow. I get tired of Wilma talking about herself all the time."

The next day, before she sat down with Cathy for dinner, Hallie walked over to where Jimmy and his brother were standing. "I forgot and made an extra sandwich. I can't eat two. Do you want it?"

Jimmy stared at Hallie a long time. Then he reached up and took the sandwich and handed it to his brother. He didn't thank Hallie, but he didn't bother her that day. After that, Hallie brought a second sandwich every week or two. Hallie was aware that she couldn't bring extra food every day. After all, the Turners didn't have much themselves. More important, Hallie knew what it was like to be poor. And she knew the poor had pride.

chapter seven

The Offer

One afternoon in late October when Hallie stopped at the Carlson farm to pick up Benny, Mrs. Carlson invited the Turners to stay for supper. Tom was already at the farm, working for Mr. Carlson. "We're having chicken and dumplings," Mrs. Carlson said.

"Oh boy, chicken and dumplings," Hallie said.

"Oh boy," Benny repeated.

"Do you want me to help?" Hallie asked.

"Perhaps you could set the table. The tablecloth is in that drawer. The silverware is in the drawer above it." She pointed at the cupboard.

"I'll help," Tessie said.

"Me too," Benny added.

Hallie took out a cloth that had big red cherries printed on it and flung it over the table. She handed Tessie the forks and Benny the spoons and kept the knives for herself. She took six plates from the cupboard and set them on the table. She set out the knives, then told Tessie and Benny to put the forks and spoons on either side of the plates. The two children mixed up the silverware, sometimes putting two spoons by one plate or setting the forks and spoons on the same side of the plates. But Hallie didn't correct them. She supposed the Carlsons were as used to misplaced silverware as she and Tom were.

Mrs. Carlson looked at the table and smiled. "Perfect," she said. "Now, who wants to ring the dinner bell?"

"I do," Tessie said.

"I do," Benny added.

"Both of us," Tessie said.

The two children went outside to ring the bell, while Hallie sliced tomatoes and bread and Mrs. Carlson dished up green beans. Hallie set the pot of chicken and dumplings on the table. Even in the good days in Oklahoma, she had never seen such a feast. "We'll stretch our stomachs," she whispered to Tom as he came into the room.

Mr. Carlson said grace, then they passed around the supper. The Carlsons, along with Tom and Hallie, helped the little ones dish up food. "Oh boy," Benny said again.

When they were finished eating, Hallie and Mrs. Carlson cleared the plates. Then Mrs. Carlson took out a rhubarb pie from the refrigerator. Hallie exchanged a glance with Tom. She couldn't remember when they last had pie. Mrs. Carlson brought out cups and saucers and poured coffee. Then she poured milk for Tessie and Benny and placed a spoonful of coffee in each of their glasses. She handed them to the children so they could pretend they had coffee, too.

It might have been the best meal Hallie had eaten in her entire life, and she told Mrs. Carlson that. She rose and started collecting the plates. Mrs. Carlson told her to sit down. "Mr. Carlson and I have something important we want to discuss with you."

As she returned to her seat, Hallie had a sinking feeling. Mr. Carlson had said he was going to tear down the hired man's cabin one day so that he could plant on the site. Maybe "one day" had come. Maybe the Carlsons felt bad about asking them to leave and were being extra nice about it. That would explain why the Turners had been invited to dinner. If that was so, Hallie hoped they could at least stay on through the winter, maybe even until school was over. They would leave for California in the spring.

She exchanged a glance with Tom, who looked wary, too. He shrugged.

"That old cabin, it ain't much, and come winter, it will get awful cold," Mr. Carlson began.

Hallie looked down at her plate. *No matter what, I'm not going to cry*, she thought. *The Carlsons have been good to us. If they tell us it's time to move on, I'm still going to be grateful.*

"Well, we worry about you down there in the winter. No heat but the cook stove. No running water," he continued.

Mrs. Carlson looked over at Hallie and saw that the girl was worried. "You do go on, Swede. It isn't about the cabin at all. Now don't worry them. Here's what we have to say. We were thinking maybe you would like to move in with us. We have all this room. Hallie could sleep with Tessie, and we can put a bed in the sewing room for Tom and Benny. We're concerned about the three of you living in the cabin. It makes no sense for you to stay there, what with us having this big house. Tessie's our only child. We never had any more, and I doubt we will now. It would be a pleasure having you children with us."

"You want to adopt us?" Tom asked. He smiled a little.

"Well, no, not exactly. But we will think of you as part of our family."

Tom and Hallie exchanged a glance. Hallie thought how nice it would be living with the Carlsons. They'd sleep in real beds and eat suppers like the one they had just finished. Still, something about the offer wasn't quite right. She and Tom and Benny had been on their own for a long time. They didn't know when they left Oklahoma if they would last a week. Now it had been almost a year. Times had been difficult, but they hadn't given up. They had endured hardships and hunger. They had not known where their next nickel would come from. But they had managed to keep going. Hallie had developed strengths she never knew she had. So had Tom. They hadn't let anybody take advantage of them.

The Carlsons had been good to them, and the offer was generous. Hallie couldn't deny that. But what if later on, the Carlsons changed their minds? Maybe Tessie and Benny wouldn't get along. Or Mrs. Carlson might become tired of having the three Turners underfoot. If they had to leave, they would be worse off than ever. Especially Benny. He'd be hurt. He wouldn't understand that although folks meant well, sometimes things didn't turn out the way one hoped they would. They had already had too many disappointments. Hallie couldn't stand another one.

Hallie glanced at Tom. To her surprise, she thought he was ready to accept. She shook her head just the slightest bit. Tom frowned. "Maybe we ought to talk this over outside," he said. He and Hallie went out to the porch where the Carlsons couldn't overhear them. "I think it's a good idea," he said.

"Not me," Hallie told him. "What if after we move in, they don't like us?"

"Aw, come on, Hallie. They know us pretty well. Nothing's going to happen."

"It might. What if Benny and Tessie have a fight? You know he can get mad sometimes. Maybe they'll think the house is too crowded? We don't know if we can all get along."

Tom smiled at his sister. "It'll be okay."

"What if it isn't, Tom? If they ask us to leave, where will we go? It's almost winter. We can't live in the car again."

Tom thought that over. "I'm tired of worrying about making enough money to support us, Hallie. I earn enough to buy school supplies and new clothes. We eat better than we used to. We even have warm blankets now. But what if I lose my job at the garage? How would we live if we don't move in with the Carlsons?"

Hallie shook her head. "You won't lose it. You're too good a mechanic. Besides, we've made it by ourselves so far."

"I thought you wanted a home."

"I do. More than anything, but I want *our* home, not the Carlsons' home." She paused. "Please, Tom."

Tom studied his sister for a long time. Then his shoulders dropped and he nodded. "If that's what you want."

The two went back inside, and Tom cleared his throat. "Nobody's ever been as good to us as you folks," he said. "We wouldn't have made it without you. So we appreciate your offer more than we can say. But I don't believe we can accept. You see, we've gotten awful independent and ornery since we've been on our own. I'd be afraid living under your roof wouldn't work out, and then we'd have to move on. I wouldn't ever want that to happen."

Tom looked to Hallie for approval. She gave a slight nod.

"We never knew anybody as kind as you. I hope you won't think we're not grateful," she said.

"No such a thing," Mrs. Carlson replied. "Swede, I told you they were independent." She turned to Hallie. "We'll think of you as neighbors then, the best neighbors we ever had." She stood up. "Let's us do the dishes, Hallie. Do you want to wash or dry?"

As they walked home later that night, Tom said, "I sure hope you're right about this. The Carlsons would be our family."

"We already are a family, our own family," Hallie said. "I think we've done a pretty good job on our own."

"How about that, Ben?" Tom asked. "You think we've done a good job?"

"Okay," Benny said.

Supper Guests

On a crisp November afternoon, Hallie and Benny walked into town to meet Tom after work at the garage. Tom's hours were eight in the morning until five at night and sometimes longer when he was repairing a car. He'd long since replaced the transmission on the Model T. Still he didn't drive the car unless he had to because he wanted to save money on gasoline. The walk was nice, he said.

Hallie liked Mr. Ulman. He didn't mind if she and Benny stopped by. Sometimes Mr. Ulman even gave Benny a penny and told him to go across the street and buy a piece of candy. So on Saturdays, Hallie and Benny often went into town to meet their brother.

That day, it took a long time to walk the mile to the garage. Benny had to examine each rock and bug they passed. He kicked up dust until his feet were the color of the road. Several cars passed them. Benny waved to each one. Two of them stopped. The drivers asked Hallie about work. Hallie shook her head. One driver thanked her. The other stared at Benny and asked, "What's wrong with that kid?"

"Nothing," Hallie replied. She muttered, "What a stupid question."

"Don't say 'stupid,'" Benny told her.

Hallie grinned at the little boy.

When they reached the station, they saw Harold's Terraplane coupe parked at the gas pump, with Harold and Dan sitting in it. Tom was filling the car's tank with gas. Hallie and Benny stood in the shade, out of sight, admiring the automobile. It was dirty, but it still shone in the harsh sunlight. Harold had the top down. Hallie thought the car looked swell. She wondered if the leather seats were hot from the sun.

"Hey, boy, you spilled gas on my car," Harold yelled, after Tom finished. He was putting the cap back on the gas tank.

Hallie had been watching closely and knew that Tom hadn't spilled. Still, he took a rag and wiped the area around the cap. Then he washed the car windows. He used a towel to polish them until they shone.

When Tom was finished, Harold said, "You missed a spot, boy."

Tom stiffened. Hallie knew he was angry at being called "boy." He didn't say anything, however. She almost wished he'd reach into the car and punch Harold. Of course he didn't dare. He would lose his job if he did. Instead, Tom glared at Harold, his fists clenched. Hallie, holding Benny's hand, stepped out into the sunlight and came to stand next to her older brother. "You got a big dent in your fender," she told Harold.

"Well, look at that. The squatter girl can see. Aren't you the bright one!"

Tom took a quick step toward the car, but Hallie grabbed his arm. "Leave be. He's not worth it. He's just a jerk."

"Who you calling a jerk?" Harold opened the door of the car and stepped out. He glared at Hallie.

Tom narrowed his eyes. "Don't you touch my sister!"

Dan smiled a little at Hallie and said, "Aw, can it, Harold."

Harold looked Tom up and down, sizing him up. Tom was bigger. He was stronger, too, because of the heavy farm work he did. Harold sneered at Tom and then got back into the car. "She's not worth it. She's just a piece of stupid trash."

"Don't say 'stupid,'" Benny said.

Harold looked at the little boy. "There's that kid."

"So what? Let's get out of here," Dan said.

"Yeah. We're wasting time." Harold leaned over the car door and said, "Go on back to Oklahoma. This isn't your home. You better keep a sharp watch behind you. We'll catch up with you one day." He pulled away, coming within inches of Hallie. She heard Harold laugh as the car sped down the road.

"The way he drives, he's liable to wreck that car," Tom said.

"Why does he hate us?" Hallie asked as she watched the Hudson disappear.

Tom shook his head.

"I'll tell you why," Mr. Ulman said. Hallie hadn't seen him come out of the garage. She hoped he wasn't angry with Tom. After all, Harold and his father were customers. The garage needed customers to stay in business. Mr. Ulman put his hand on Benny's head and said, "Hi, Benny."

He turned back to Hallie. "I'll tell you," he repeated. "Harold has no self-respect. He's never worked a day in his life. Funny thing is I bet he wishes Tom was his friend. I believe he admires Tom."

Tom shook his head and muttered, "I doubt it."

"No. I believe he does. That boy knows you're a better man."

"What about Dan?" Hallie asked. "Is he that way, too?"

"Oh, Dan is all right by himself, but he doesn't have a backbone. I think hanging around with Harold makes him feel important." Mr. Ulman took a rag from his back pocket and wiped a smudge on the gas pump. "I got to say I admire you, too, Tom, you and your sister."

"Not everybody does," Hallie told him. "Some people tell us to git. They say we ought to go back to where we came from."

"These are hard times. I'd tell Harold to take his business elsewhere, but I can't afford to. I need the money. And you need the job, Tom. That's why you didn't punch him. For a minute there, I thought you would. I wouldn't have blamed you, but I'd have had to fire you." He swatted Tom with the towel, then stuffed it back into his pocket. As he turned to go, he spotted an old car that was pulling to a stop. It was loaded down with a family and belongings. Mr. Ulman shook his head. "Everybody's got it tough," he said.

Hallie looked at the car, too. Mattresses were tied to the roof with rope. Piled on top of them were chairs and a battered trunk. A man sat in the driver's seat. Beside him was a sad-faced woman holding a baby. She looked as if she hadn't slept in days. Two children sat in the back seat. They looked tired and dirty. Their faces were thin. Hallie knew they were hungry.

Sometimes strangers thought she was from the town, and they stopped and asked her about work. Their cars were as worn out as the Turners' Model T. Usually it was the man who asked. Occasionally it was a tired-faced woman, holding a baby who was whining from the heat and dust. The back seat was often filled with kids. Their faces were as dirty as their clothes. Even the children had a look of despair. Hallie knew she and her brothers had looked like this before they met the Carlsons. She hated telling people that she didn't know of any work. The man would nod and say, "Thank you just the same." If he hadn't given up hope, he might swear under his breath. More often, he nodded. He'd known before he asked what the answer would be. Then the car would lumber off down the road. Hallie would thank her lucky stars that Tom had work and they had a place to live. In the back of her mind, however, was the thought that at any time, their luck could turn. They, too, could be back on the road, headed for California.

Now as Hallie and Tom stared at the old Chevrolet, the man got out and lifted the hood and unscrewed the radiator cap. Steam poured out, and he jumped back. He kicked a tire that was low. The man seemed to be too tired to put much effort into the kick. He slowly walked toward the garage. His overalls were ragged and dirty, and his shoulders sagged. He looked defeated by life. The woman and children watched him.

"Say, mister, I got a problem with my wheel. I'd sure appreciate it if you could take a look," the man told Tom.

Hallie winced when the man called Tom "mister." He was probably twenty years older than Tom.

"I got to be honest. I don't have no money to pay you with."

Tom looked at Mr. Ulman, who shrugged. "Go ahead.

We don't charge to look."

"Seems like you could use water in that radiator, too," Tom said, picking up a watering can. "Is the tire flat?"

"I hope that's all. A couple of young fellows come roaring by me a minute ago. Real nice car they had, a convertible. I swerved to miss them and went in the ditch. The tire pret' near blowed, and I think the wheel's maybe wrenched."

"Can you pull it over here?" Tom asked.

"Yes, sir. I think that tire'll make it. I sure do appreciate it." The man held out his hand. "Name's Trigg. Curtis Trigg."

"Tom Turner."

"I'm Benny."

"Well, hello there, squirt." Mr. Trigg smiled for the first time. Then he turned to Tom. "We knew Turners in Oklahoma."

"We're from Oklahoma," Hallie spoke up. "Near Cookietown."

Mr. Trigg looked surprised. "That's where we hail from, north of it a bit."

His wife had gotten out of the car and walked across the road, her children behind her. "I knew a Mrs. Selena Turner that's went to the church. I was there once or twice but Pa didn't take to it," she said.

"That's our mother," Hallie told her.

"I heard of a Trigg boy. He was older than me, maybe twenty," Tom said.

"That'd be our Charlie. He's gone now, went off to California. We ain't heard from him since we got dusted out. Ain't heard from the other kids neither. We got two more boys that went off. But we got three young ones with us. That's Etta and Jim, and I got the baby. We ain't named him yet."

"You looking for a job?" Mr. Ulman asked Mr. Trigg.

"You said it, mister. We heard there's work over west of here. That's where we're headed. You know anything about that?"

Both Tom and Mr. Ulman shook their heads.

"Maybe we'll go on to California, that is if old Betsy here can make it." When Tom looked puzzled, the man said, "Betsy. That's what we call this flivver."

"We were on our way to California when we stopped here," Hallie told Mrs. Trigg. "We're staying for a while." She added, "We hope."

Mr. Trigg went back across the road, started the car, and

pulled it into the station. Hallie could see that the tire was low. "It needs a patch, all right," Tom said. *From the looks of it, the patch would have to go on top of another patch,* Hallie thought. She wondered how long it would be before the tire simply gave out.

Tom crawled under the car to check on the wheel. Mrs. Trigg went inside the station, her children following after her. She found a broom and began sweeping the floor. "If we can't pay you, at least we can clean up a little. You got some rags and a bucket? Me and Etta will wash the window," Mrs. Trigg told Mr. Ulman. Hallie and Benny stood in the doorway, watching.

Mr. Ulman shook his head. "You don't have—"

"No, sir. We pay our way the best we can. Come on, kids. We'll scrub the floor, too."

The children were young, younger than Benny, but they pitched in. In a minute, Benny said, "I'll help. I'm a good helper." He found a rag and wiped it across a chair. Hallie picked up a scrub brush and started on the grime on the door.

"I think I remember your mama. She's a right nice woman. Pretty, too, plump as cotton," Mrs. Trigg said.

"She got thin."

"Well, who hasn't?" Mrs. Trigg asked. "How's she doing?"

Hallie scrubbed hard at the door and didn't answer for a moment. "She died before we left."

Mrs. Trigg stopped washing the window and looked at Hallie. "I'm real sorry for that. I'd of gone to her service if I'd of knowed. We lost two of ours. I couldn't hardly stand to stay in the house after that. I'd look over at where they slept and forget for a minute they weren't there. I didn't mind so much later on that we got dusted out." She was silent for a moment, then smiled. "I guess we got to forget the sorrow and look at what we got."

Like what? Hallie wanted to ask, but she didn't. After all, there were things to be grateful for, she thought, looking at Benny. He was rubbing his dirty dust rag over the top of the papers on a table, leaving them smudged.

She smiled at her brother, who looked up and said, "I'm helping, Hallie."

"He's a worker," Mrs. Trigg said.

Hallie liked the woman. She seemed hardworking and friendly, and none of the Triggs had asked what was wrong with Benny. "We'd be proud to have you stay for supper,"

Hallie said suddenly. "We live in a cabin down the road. We don't have much, but we'd be glad to share."

"Ain't nobody asked us to supper since we left," the woman said. "We'd be mighty glad for it."

Tom came into the office then and said the wheel was all right. The only problem was the tire. He could patch it, but . . . He shook his head. When Hallie told him she'd invited the Triggs for supper, he nodded his approval. "I was thinking the same," he said.

Hallie told them she'd go on home, then, and start supper. Just before she left, Mr. Ulman came into the station office. "I've went to the mercantile. I thought your kids might like this," he said. He handed Mrs. Trigg a box of Cracker Jack.

~

Mrs. Trigg examined every inch of the Turners' cabin. "I always thought a curtain made a window look pretty. Look how the sunlight comes through it," she said, fingering the fabric. She admired the pots and pans and dishes on the bureau. She gently touched the china bowl that had belonged to Mommy. "I used to have such. I had to leave them behind," she said. "They'd be broke if I hadn't."

She ran her hand over the iron bedstead that had been in the cabin when the Turners moved in and sighed. "My, to sleep in a real bed again."

Mommy's blue-and-white quilt hanging on the wall really caught her eye, however. "The finest I ever seen," she said. She examined her hand to make sure it was clean. Then she ran it over the quilt. "Was there ever a woman couldn't help but touch a piece of material?"

"You quilt, Mrs. Trigg?" Hallie asked.

"My yes, girl. You want to see? Etta, go get Mama's New York Beauty and them from the car."

The little girl ran out and returned with an armful of quilts. She held them carefully.

"I couldn't leave them behind," Mrs. Trigg said, spreading them out on the bed.

Hallie still didn't know much about quilts, but she could see these were almost as well made as Mommy's.

"You quilt, too, do you?" Mrs. Trigg asked.

"I'm just learning," Hallie replied. "Our neighbor, Mrs. Carlson, is teaching me."

"Then you are in for a lifetime of pleasures."

Hallie ran her hand over Mrs. Trigg's New York Beauty. It was made mostly from feed sacks. She touched a yellow square.

"I knowed you'd see that. I bought it at the store, a whole yard of it. It's the best quality there is, and it cost me a quarter. Imagine spending all that money on material. Back then, I didn't give it a thought. Now I could sure use that quarter. Still . . ." Her voice drifted off, and Hallie knew that Mrs. Trigg was glad she actually had the fabric. "I still got a little piece of it left. On a bad day, it makes me happy to see it."

Hallie went back to preparing supper. As usual there were beans and corn bread, but she had tomatoes and lettuce and fresh milk from the Carlsons. She'd expected the vegetables to last a week, but she didn't mind sharing them with the Triggs. There were apples, too. *'A' for 'apple pie,'* Hallie thought, as she cut up the apples and set them into a crust.

When all was ready, both families took their plates out into the yard because there wasn't enough room for all of them at the table. Mr. Trigg asked the blessing. Then everyone ate quickly, not talking until they were done.

" 'Bout the best supper I ever ate," Mr. Trigg said, using a piece of corn bread to wipe his plate.

"We ain't ate like this since I can't remember," Mrs. Trigg said. "You folks sure have been good to us."

Hallie exchanged a glance with Tom. They were both proud that with Tom's earnings, they could afford to buy good food—and to share it with others.

After Etta and Mrs. Trigg helped Hallie wash the dishes, Tom said the Triggs were welcome to stay the night. He pointed to the spot where he and Hallie and Benny had first camped. "I stopped by the Carlsons' on the way home, and they said it was all right."

"We can't thank you folks enough," Mr. Trigg said. "You and Mr. Ulman. Like the Bible says, you taken us in when we was hungry."

Tom had persuaded Mr. Ulman to give the Triggs a used tire that had been lying behind the garage. It was old, but it was better than the one Tom had patched.

Tom and Benny, along with Mr. Trigg and his boy, set up the Trigg tent. As soon as it was dark, they all went to bed.

In the morning, the Triggs were gone.

"Why did they leave so early? I was going to fix them breakfast," Hallie said.

"They didn't want to be beholden," Tom told her. "They

left the place clean as a whistle. You'd never know anybody was camped here."

Benny was disappointed the children were gone. He called to them and said, "Don't hide." Then he went over to a tree and removed something hanging from a branch. "Look, Hallie. They forgot." He handed her a piece of yellow fabric.

"Mrs. Trigg sure will be sorry she forgot that," Tom said.

Hallie took the fabric from Benny and shook her head. "Mrs. Trigg didn't forget. She left it on purpose. Giving us her fabric is her way of thanking us."

chapter nine

Ragman

"No school," Benny said when Hallie walked him home from the Carlsons' farm one afternoon late in the fall.

"You're right. There's no school tomorrow," Hallie told him.

"No school. No more school." He stopped to pick a dried flower, then held it out to Hallie. She reached for it. Benny pulled it back and began plucking the flower strands and throwing them into the wind.

"You love school, Benny."

"No!" he shouted, then ran ahead of Hallie down the road.

She caught up with him. "What are you talking about, Benny? Don't you want to go back to school? Did something happen today?"

"I saw Bob," Benny told her.

"You saw Bob at school?"

"No. That's stupid."

Benny never used that word because he knew it was cruel. Now he stamped his foot in frustration when Hallie didn't understand him. "No school!" he said.

Hallie had rarely seen her little brother angry. He got frustrated with himself sometimes. That was usually when he couldn't perform a task he'd set out to do. He rarely was angry at other people. Now he was mad, and Hallie didn't understand why.

"Look! Bob!" he called, forgetting for a moment that he was upset. He pointed to the bushes. Hallie didn't see a rabbit. "Where's Bob?" Hallie asked.

"There, stupid!"

"Benny!" Hallie said. "That's a bad word." He never before had called her stupid.

"Tessie's stupid," he said.

"Tessie's your friend."

"No," Benny said. "Not my friend."

"Did you have a fight?" Hallie asked. Mrs. Carlson had said nothing about a falling-out between the two. In fact, Mrs. Carlson was pleased that both children had recognized the letters on a set of alphabet blocks she had purchased at the general store.

Benny didn't answer. When Hallie asked him again, he said, "Don't talk."

By the time they reached home, Benny didn't say anything more about Tessie and their school. Hallie hoped that he had forgotten why he was upset. When Tom arrived, he asked Benny how school had gone, and Benny, angry, said only, "No."

"What happened?" Tom asked Hallie.

She shook her head. "I can't get it out of him. He'll probably forget whatever it was. So let's not remind him."

They didn't talk about school or about Tessie until bedtime. As they knelt beside the bed for prayers, Hallie told Benny to ask God to keep Tessie and the Carlsons safe. "No," he said.

"Why not."

"Tessie likes Ragman. Ragman's stupid."

"Who's Ragman?"

"Ragman," was all Benny would say.

"Ragman?" Tom asked when Hallie told him what Benny had said. "Do you suppose Ragman is some hobo? I haven't seen anyone snooping around the place, and Mr. Carlson hasn't hired anybody besides me."

"Maybe he's a relative. Does Tessie have any cousins?"

"Not that I've seen. I'm sure Benny will forget by tomorrow."

Hallie wasn't sure. She'd never seen Benny so agitated.

She was right. In the morning, the little boy was still in a dark mood. He banged his spoon against the table and said he didn't like corn bread. Hallie tried to talk to him, but he refused to say what was wrong. Something surely had happened at his school the day before. Hallie couldn't imagine what, though. The idea of teaching the children together had been a wonderful one. Benny and Tessie learned from each other, and Mrs. Carlson's watching over Benny allowed Hallie herself to go to school. The two children had gotten along and everything seemed to be working so well that Hallie no longer worried about not completing eighth grade. If Benny refused to go to school, however, Hallie would have to drop out. She had to find out what was wrong with him.

Tom stayed home with his brother the next day, so after school Hallie stopped by the Carlson place. She told Mrs. Carlson about Benny. "Did Benny have a fight with Tessie?" Hallie asked.

"Not that I know of. They always get along so well together," Mrs. Carlson replied. "If they did have a disagreement, Tessie didn't say anything." She called the little girl into the room. "Did you play with Benny yesterday?"

Tessie frowned, then said she couldn't remember.

"Benny doesn't want to have school anymore," Mrs. Carlson told her daughter.

"Okay," Tessie said. She was singing to a doll that her mother had made for her and didn't pay attention to either Mrs. Carlson or Hallie.

"Was Benny mean to you?" Hallie asked.

"I like Benny."

Hallie was quiet for a moment, trying to remember what Benny had said. Then she asked, "Who's Ragman?"

"Ragman?" Mrs. Carlson asked.

"Benny said something about Ragman. He said that

Tessie liked him."

Mrs. Carlson shook her head. "There's been nobody by that name here. In fact, there's been nobody here at all." She frowned. "We get tramps sometimes. Do you suppose . . ." She drew in her breath. "I try to never let her out of my sight." Then she turned to her daughter and asked gently, "Tessie, have you seen a man around here?"

"Tom," Tessie replied.

"Another man, a man we don't know?"

"No."

"Would she remember?" Hallie asked.

"She might not." Mrs. Carlson shook her head. "If someone had been here, he must be gone by now. I'll ask Mr. Carlson to watch out for anybody trespassing, although he does so already."

"I hate to think somebody was scaring Benny," Hallie said.

"What about those visitors you had? You don't think . . . ?" Mrs. Carlson asked.

"They pulled out days ago. We haven't seen a trace of them since. Besides, they were real nice folks."

"From now on, we'll keep a sharp watch. I surely do

not like the idea there is a stranger around." She thought a minute, then asked, "Do you think Benny made him up? I know sometimes he talks about a Bob."

Hallie laughed. "Bob was our rabbit. Every time he sees a rabbit, he thinks it's Bob."

Mrs. Carlson laughed, too. "That explains that. I always wondered." Then she asked, "Do you think there's a connection between Bob and Ragman?"

"Not that I know of."

Mrs. Carlson had been kneading bread dough. She used her hands to push the dough back and forth on the oilcloth-covered table. She added flour when the dough began to stick. When she finished, she punched down the dough with her fist, then dropped it into an oiled bowl. She covered the bowl with a damp towel. The day was muggy, and she wiped her forehead with the back of her hand, leaving streaks of flour. "Dough rises funny on a damp day like this," she said. "How's your cook stove work for bread?"

"Better than a fireplace."

"I never could get the hang of baking bread in that old thing. The bread was either raw or burned. That's why I got in the habit of buying store-made. But Mr. Carlson likes a homemade bread. He says if he knew how much better the bread would be from a gas stove, he'd have bought me one years ago." She pushed the bowl away from her and sat down. "But we're not talking about bread."

Hallie pulled out another chair and sat down, too. "No."

"How serious is this? Do you think Benny will get over Ragman, whoever he is?"

"I don't know. I've never seen him stay mad like this."

"It's a shame. He and Tessie are such friends. They learn from each other. I can't tell you how many times I've tried to explain something to Tessie, but she doesn't understand. Then Benny says something, and all of a sudden she gets it."

"It works the other way, too. Tessie told him words are made up of all the letters in the alphabet. He understood. I thought that was pretty smart of her."

"They bring out the best in each other. Tessie's never been so happy."

"Benny, either."

"We'll have to figure something out. Your education's at stake here, too, Hallie."

Hallie knew that was true. When she reached home, Tom told her that Benny had been in a bad mood all day.

He walked into the creek with his shoes on. When Tom saw a rabbit and said, "There's Bob," Benny had said that Bob was stupid. "I don't get it. He's always been so happy. What do you suppose caused this?" Tom asked.

Hallie only shook her head.

She stayed home from school the next day to take care of Benny. He was not as grumpy, but neither was he happy. Hallie tried to get him to sing "Happy Days Are Here Again," but Benny refused. She suggested fishing. The little boy loved to fish, even though he never caught anything. He was just happy to sit on a stream bank with his fishing pole and call, "Here, fish." But now Benny shook his head and replied, "No fish."

That night when Tom came home from the Carlson farm, Benny was still in a sour mood. "I talked to Mr. Carlson. He can't figure out what's wrong, either. Whatever it is, Tessie's fine. When I saw her, she was sitting on a blanket in the yard singing her doll to sleep. I asked if I could hold it, but she wouldn't let me. At least she has that for company. I told Mrs. Carlson to bring her over here tomorrow. Maybe that will make a difference. We'd see what's going on with the two of them."

Later that evening, as she was washing dishes, Hallie heard a car stop. They were used to the sounds of cars going past on the road, but it wasn't often that one stopped.

"Somebody must have seen the light and wants to inquire about work. I'll check," Tom said.

Hallie hoped that was who it was. From time to time, she saw single men walking through the woods. They scared her, especially if she was alone with Benny. Who knew what a stranger might do?

"It's Mr. Carlson," Tom called. "Evening, sir. Come on in."

Thinking he might want coffee, Hallie poured water into the tea kettle. She checked the grounds in the coffeepot, trying to remember how many times they had been used. Maybe she should throw them out and put in fresh. "I can make coffee," she said when Mr. Carlson came inside.

"No need. It sours my stomach at night."

Hallie remembered he'd turned down coffee the night they met him, too.

Mr. Carlson looked around for Benny and saw him curled up on the bed. "Hi there, Benny. I should have brought Tessie along."

Benny didn't reply.

"Well, you'll see her in the morning. Mrs. Carlson said to tell you she's bringing Tessie over here tomorrow. Tessie's looking forward to seeing you."

"Tessie doesn't like me," Benny said.

"Of course she does. You're her best friend."

"No," Benny said.

Mr. Carlson turned to Hallie. "I stopped to tell you that Mrs. Carlson wants you to know that everything will be all right. She's got it all figured out."

"What is it?" Hallie asked.

Mr. Carlson shook his head. "She'll tell you when she gets here."

"Does she know who Ragman is?"

"As to that, I can't say. She just told me to tell you she knows what's wrong and that Benny will be fine."

After Mr. Carlson left, Hallie said, "He could have told us what happened."

"Maybe he doesn't know."

"I bet he does," Hallie told her brother. "He acted like it was some kind of surprise."

"Well, I hope for Benny's sake it's a nice surprise."

"No," Benny told Hallie in the morning when she announced that Tessie was coming to the cabin.

"Everything will be all right, Benny. Tessie's your friend."

"No. She's Ragman's friend. I hate Ragman."

"Benny!" She'd never heard Benny use the word "hate." In fact, Benny liked almost everybody. Who was this Ragman who had caused so much trouble? She hoped Mrs. Carlson had indeed figured it out. Benny ate breakfast and then went outside and began playing with building blocks that Tom had made for him out of scraps of wood he'd found at the filling station.

"Do you think Tessie can count how many blocks there are?" Hallie asked. Benny had learned to count to nine, the number of the blocks.

"No."

Hallie heard the sound of an engine and looked up to see the Carlsons' car. Tessie opened the back door and jumped out. "Hi, Benny," she said.

Benny frowned and looked at his blocks instead of Tessie.

"I brought my doll," she said, but Benny turned his head away.

Mrs. Carlson got out of the car with a brown paper sack in her arms. "I have a surprise for you, Benny," she said.

At the word "surprise," Benny forgot he was angry and looked up at Mrs. Carlson. "What is it?"

"Mama made it for you," Tessie said. She was excited and jumped up and down with her doll in her arms.

Benny glanced at the doll and looked away.

"Do you want to see the surprise?" Mrs. Carlson asked.

"Okay," Benny said.

Mrs. Carlson handed Benny the sack. He reached into it and took out something wrapped in tissue paper and tied with a ribbon. "A present," he said.

"It's for you," Tessie told him.

Benny tore off the tissue and found himself holding a rag doll with bright red hair and button eyes. "Ragman!" he cried.

"It's yours to keep," Mrs. Carlson said. "His name is Andy."

Benny stared at the doll for a moment, then grinned. "Look, Tessie. I have Ragman. *My* Ragman."

Hallie and Tom exchanged a glance, then turned to Mrs. Carlson. "Ragman?" they asked together.

She smiled. "I tried and tried to think who Ragman was. Then as I was putting Tessie down for her nap, she asked me to hold the Raggedy Ann doll. I'd just made it for her. I gave it to her the night before Benny came for school the last time. Tessie slurred the words, and they came out 'Rag-Ann.' That's when I realized Ragman was really Raggedy Ann. Tessie had played with the doll the entire time Benny was there that day. I guess she ignored him, and maybe she even told him the doll was her friend. I remembered then that they didn't play with each other most of the day. Perhaps Tessie told Benny she wanted to play with Raggedy Ann instead of him. When I asked Tessie about it, she didn't remember. I thought if I made a similar doll for Benny, that would solve the problem."

"I think it has," Hallie said. She looked over at the two children, who were holding the dolls.

"Hi, Ragman," Tessie said.

"Hi, Ragman," Benny repeated.

Both children burst into giggles.

chapter ten

Christmas

"Santa Claus is coming," Benny announced one day in December.

"Who's Santa Claus?" Tom teased.

Benny looked confused. "Santa Claus."

"I don't think he remembers," Hallie said. The three of them had been on the road the winter before and hadn't had the money for presents. So they had skipped Christmas. "Who told you about Santa Claus?" Hallie asked Benny.

"Tessie."

"What did she say?"

"He brings stockings."

Hallie smiled. "Does he put something in stockings?" she asked.

"Feet," Benny answered. Hallie and Tom burst out laughing, and Benny joined them.

Later Hallie told Tom, "Santa's going to bring a present to Tessie. We'll have to get something for Benny."

Tom looked away. With the harvest over, he no longer worked for Mr. Carlson. They were now living on what Tom made from his work at the garage. Money was tight. After they paid for food and kerosene and sometimes splurged on a moving picture show, there was little left over. The Carlsons were generous with food and things for the cabin, but the Turners couldn't ask them for money.

"Benny needs a new jacket," Hallie said.

"So do I," Tom told her. "I left mine someplace."

Hallie glanced at her brother. It wasn't like him to lose anything.

"Maybe I can do without. I still have Daddy's warm sweater," Tom said.

Hallie shook her head. The weather had already turned cold. Tom had chinked the cabin, spreading mud in the spaces between the logs to keep out the wind and cold air.

They kept a fire going in the cook stove on the days they spent in the cabin. There was ice in the creek in the mornings when Tom went to fetch water. Snow threatened. "We have enough money in the purse for your jacket," Hallie said.

"No, Benny comes first."

"I'll order Benny's jacket from the Sears, Roebuck wish book at the mercantile on my way home from school," she said. She'd order a jacket for Tom, too. It would be a surprise for Christmas.

"I wish we had something else for Benny," Hallie said.

"There's an old scooter behind the garage. It must have fallen off somebody's car. I found it on the road. Nobody's claimed it. I'll fix it up for Benny."

"He can use it to chase Bob." Hallie laughed.

She thought about other presents. She would make a corn husk doll for Tessie. She had learned to do that in Oklahoma. She'd already decided to make an apron for Mrs. Carlson. The present that worried her most was the one for a schoolmate. The eighth-grade class had drawn names, and the students were supposed to give a present to the person whose name they had picked. Hallie had to give a gift to Mildred, one of Wilma's friends. The teacher said they were not to spend more than five cents on the presents. Hallie didn't have an extra five cents. Neither did many of the other students. That was why the teacher told them the best presents would be ones they made.

"I don't know what to give her," Hallie told Cathy.

"Me too," Cathy said. "I have to give something to Dorothy, and I don't want to spend even a penny on *her*." The two girls laughed. Ever since Hallie had made the remark comparing relatives to squatters, Wilma and her cousin Dorothy had all but ignored her. Of course, Hallie had made no effort to become friends with them. She knew they would reject her. *Why put myself out when they will only call me a squatter?* Once the teacher had suggested that Hallie and Wilma work together on a project showing the capitals of each state. Wilma said she'd rather work with Dorothy. The other girls stuck with Wilma, too. So Cathy was Hallie's only friend. It had been easy to make friends in Oklahoma. Hallie wondered why it had been so hard here. Maybe she didn't try hard enough, but the other kids didn't, either.

Hallie liked Cathy. She lived with her parents, two brothers, and a younger sister in a sod house on her grandparents' farm. The house was called a soddy because it was made from strips of sod or prairie grass, stacked up layer upon layer.

Hallie had taken Benny there one Saturday morning. She had been surprised that so many people could live in a house the size of their cabin. Cathy's mother had insisted Hallie and Benny stay for dinner. They sat on the bed, which was on one side of the table. "You can sit there and stir the soup on the stove," Cathy's mother had said with a laugh.

Now Hallie and Cathy sat outside the school with their dinner sacks, talking about the Christmas presents. "I don't want to give Dorothy anything at all, but that wouldn't be fair," Cathy said. "Wouldn't it be awful if everybody else got a present but you? That would be mean. And embarrassing."

Hallie agreed. "I suppose we have to go to the store and buy something. I wish we hadn't drawn names."

"Me too. At least you can sew. Maybe you can make Mildred a skirt or something."

"For five cents?" Both girls laughed.

"Dorothy likes yellow. I could give her a yellow ribbon."

Hallie brightened. "I know. I have some yellow material that a lady gave me. We could make her a yellow handkerchief. She's always carrying around a hanky. I think she'd like that. In fact, we could make handkerchiefs for both of them and embroider their names on them." She thought a minute. "Not their names, their initials. That won't take as long."

"If you donate the fabric, I'll buy the embroidery floss. It costs a lot less than five cents. That's a swell idea, Hallie. Those will be the best presents in the whole room."

A few days before Christmas, Tom, Hallie, and Benny went into the woods to chop down a Christmas tree. Mr. Carlson had given Tom permission. He told Tom, "Take any one you want. Take two. Take ten. The more the better, since I intend to plant that land one day."

"Which one do you want, Ben?" Tom asked.

"That one!" Benny shouted, pointing at the tallest evergreen in the grove.

"It's taller than our cabin. You'll have to choose a smaller one," Hallie said.

"How about that one?" Tom asked, pointing to a shorter tree.

"Okay."

Tom cut down the tree. He and Hallie dragged it to the

cabin, Benny marching in front of them. When they reached the cabin, they discovered that that tree also was too tall to go inside. So they went back to the pine grove. "Choose a small tree this time," Tom told his brother.

Benny took his time. He walked around studying each tree, pointing to several, then shaking his head each time. Finally, he put his hand on a tree that was misshapen. The trunk was bent, and one side was almost bare of branches. "There," he said.

"It's a stupid tree," Tom said.

"Don't say 'stupid.'"

"It's ugly, then."

"I know," Benny replied.

Tom chopped down the funny little tree. He dragged it to the cabin and propped it in a corner. "I never saw a Christmas tree that looked like that," Hallie said, stepping back and surveying the tree.

"I like it," Benny told her.

That evening, they cut out stars from a newspaper Tom had brought home from the station, and Benny colored them with a crayon Tessie had given him. Hallie went outside and collected dried red berries from bushes and strung them together. She took cotton batting that had come out of an old quilt and placed it on the tree to look like snow.

"There's just one more thing," she said. She told Tom and Benny to close their eyes. She went to the box where Mommy's good quilt had been stored. She took out a small bundle wrapped in newspaper. "No peeking," she said. The brothers closed their eyes until Hallie called, "Ready."

The two opened their eyes and stared at the tree. On top was a glass angel. One wing had been broken off, and the face was scratched, but it meant more to the Turners than any Christmas tree in the world. The angel had belonged to Mommy. It had been on every Christmas tree they had ever had in Oklahoma. "I knew you'd say to throw it out when we left Oklahoma, but I just couldn't," Hallie told Tom.

"I'm glad you didn't," he said.

Benny grinned at the tree. "The best Christmas tree," he declared.

~

Mrs. Carlson invited the Turners for Christmas Eve dinner, but Hallie turned down the invitation. "We want *you* to be *our* guests instead," she said.

"But our house is so much bigger, and we have a gas stove," Mr. Carlson had protested.

His wife touched his arm. "We would be pleased to accept," she said.

Later back at the cabin Tom asked Hallie, "Why'd you do that?"

"They've been so good to us. It's time to pay them back."

"With pancakes and beans?" Tom asked.

"Mrs. Carlson said they'd come only if they could give us a chicken. I'll fix stewed tomatoes and fried potatoes and applesauce from dried apples. And guess what's for desert?"

Tom shook his head.

"Divinity. I've saved enough sugar, and we'll use the black walnuts we gathered in the fall."

"Just like home," Tom said.

On Christmas Eve, the Carlsons arrived at the cabin early, since they were all going together to the service at the church and then to the school for punch and cookies. Mr. Carlson carried in a box of presents wrapped in bright paper. "You can't open them till morning," he said.

"We have presents for you, too," Tom said, pointing to two bundles wrapped in paper saved from the store and tied with string. Inside were the corn husk doll and an apron. Mr. Carlson's present was outside—a chopping block. Tom had made it from a tree stump. It would replace the worn-down block that Mr. Carlson kept beside his chicken coop.

Mr. Carlson handed Hallie a box of chocolates and said, "For our hostess."

"I made you a present," Benny told Tessie and handed her a necklace that was a string of dried berries.

"My favorite." Tessie put it over her head. "We have a present for you. Mom said don't tell it's a sweater."

They all crowded around the table for Hallie's dinner, eating quickly. When he was finished, Mr. Carlson said, "Best chicken I ever had."

"That's because it came from you," Hallie said. She collected the tin plates.

"It's sensible of you to use tin. Someone is always breaking our china dishes," Mrs. Carlson said.

"I do not," Tessie told her mother.

"I wasn't talking about you." Mrs. Carlson glanced at her husband, who blushed. Then she said, "It was an awful good dinner. I couldn't eat another thing."

"Well, you have to," Hallie said. She took a plate from the top of the bureau and set it on the table.

"Divinity candy!" Mr. Carlson said. "Well, will you look at that, Tessie."

"Yay!" Tessie said.

"Yay!" Benny repeated.

"It is indeed the best Christmas dinner we ever had," Mrs. Carlson said.

They hurried to wash the dishes so that they could reach the church before the service started. When they went outside, they discovered that snow was falling, coming down in big flakes like white butterflies. Benny and Tessie raised their faces to the sky, laughing when the flakes landed on them.

"We should have brought that old sleigh in the barn," Mr. Carlson said.

"It holds only three. That means you'd have to make two trips," his wife said. "Some of us might miss part of the service."

That would be all right with me, Hallie thought.

Hallie had tried going to church. In the fall, she had taken Benny to a service, but she felt out of place. In the middle of a prayer, Benny had pointed to a window with colored glass and said, "I like red." Worshipers had turned around and stared or frowned, and one man had laughed. Hallie had stayed home after that.

She wished they could skip the service and go just to the school, but they were with the Carlsons. Besides, Benny was excited to go. He and Tessie ran ahead of them into the church. Mrs. Carlson followed, leading the way to the front. "We always sit here. This is our pew," she said.

"We'll sit in the back," Hallie told her.

"Oh, for land sakes. You've as much right to sit in front as anyone."

Hallie shook her head. "We'd rather be back there," she said.

Mrs. Carlson seemed to understand. "I guess we'll all sit in the back, then."

As people came in, they greeted the Carlsons, then glanced at the Turners. "What are you doing way back here?"

one woman asked.

"We're sitting with our neighbors," Mrs. Carlson told her.

"The squatters?"

"No, like I said, our neighbors."

The woman frowned at her, and Hallie felt like slumping down in her seat. She wished they hadn't come. Tom, however, stood up and extended his hand. "Hi. I'm Tom Turner. This is my sister, Hallie, and my brother, Benny."

"Oh, I seen you at the garage," the woman's husband said, shaking Tom's hand.

"Good for you," Mrs. Carlson told Tom after the couple took their seats.

Other people crowded into the church then. Hallie looked down at her hands after she noticed Wilma and Dorothy. Dan and Harold came in, too. Harold spotted Tom and nudged his friend. Dan raised his hand in greeting, but Harold grabbed it. "Hey, it's Christmas," Dan said. Tom nodded at him. Cathy came down the aisle and grinned at Hallie.

The pews filled quickly, people crowded together against the cold. They kept on their heavy coats, because the stove at the front of the church did not send out much heat. Mr.

Carlson had on a warm jacket lined with sheepskin. Hallie was glad she had ordered the winter jacket for Tom. He'd be pleased when he opened his present in the morning.

The room was noisy. Worshipers greeted each other and shouted, "Merry Christmas!" A woman began playing the piano. The room grew still. When the pianist was finished, the minister stood and greeted everybody. "This is God's house, and all are welcome here," he said.

Hallie glanced around and wondered if she and Tom and Benny were truly welcome.

The congregation sang "Silent Night." Then Wilma went to the front of the room and read the story of the birth of Jesus from the Bible. She stumbled over the words, mispronouncing them. Every now and then, she rubbed her hands on her skirt. Hallie realized Wilma was nervous, just like Hallie was when she had to stand up in front of the class to recite. *I'm sorry for you, Wilma,* Hallie thought. *Now you know what it's like to have people stare at you.*

The preacher gave a short sermon explaining the meaning of Christmas. Then the congregation sang "Joy to the World."

Two men passed around collection plates. Hallie hadn't

thought about an offering and had not brought any money. She hoped nobody would notice. Tom reached into his pocket and took out a nickel. Mr. Carlson slipped a dollar into the plate. He'd folded it up so that nobody would notice the bill. He wasn't showy like others in the congregation who flashed the dollars they gave. When the collection plate reached Hallie, it wasn't very full. She saw that some people had given only a penny and she thought a few might have given nothing at all. There were more poor people in the church than rich ones, Hallie realized. She wondered if they were as uncomfortable as she was.

The minister announced the final hymn. As the pianist started to play, Benny shouted, "Sing 'Happy Days'!"

Mrs. Carlson smiled. Mr. Carlson laughed out loud. Hallie turned red and stared straight ahead, wondering if Wilma and Dorothy were looking at her.

"Yeah, 'Happy Days,'" Tessie repeated.

It seemed to Hallie that everyone in the congregation turned to stare at them. One man grinned at Benny, but a few glared. One woman looked at the Turners for a moment and then shook her head.

The minister was among those who smiled. "As the Bible

tells us, a little child shall lead them," he said. "Yes, son, these are happy days when we come together to praise the Lord on His birthday. But I think we'll sing 'O Come, All Ye Faithful' instead."

"Okay," Benny said.

When the song was over, the congregation hurried through the snow to the school next door. Tom and Benny went with the Carlsons to the room where refreshments were being served. Hallie found Cathy, and the two went to their classroom. Presents with the students' names on them were piled on the teacher's desk. They had been brought the day before. When everyone was there, Mrs. Powell handed out the gifts, and the students unwrapped them. Hallie watched as Dorothy opened her present and said, "Wow. I love yellow. Thanks whoever made this!" Dorothy looked around until she saw Cathy smiling at her. The presents were anonymous, but the students seemed to figure out who they were from anyway.

Then Mildred opened her present and frowned. "I don't like hankies. I wonder who gave it to me." Hallie ducked her head. When she looked up, Mildred was staring at her.

Cathy had already opened her present—a bright blue

hair ribbon. Now Hallie tore off the paper on her gift and found a yellow pencil.

"That's nice," Cathy said. "Somebody must like you."

Hallie didn't respond. She noticed that two other children had yellow pencils, too. She knew who had bought them—Mrs. Powell. Hallie had seen the pencils on the teacher's desk the day before. Mrs. Powell had bought several of them. They were for students who didn't receive presents. Someone had drawn Hallie's name and was too mean to bring her a gift. She wondered if it had been Wilma.

chapter eleven

Harold

Winter was difficult for everyone.

One day after school started in January, Hallie made an extra bean sandwich to give to Jimmy. Mrs. Carlson had shared a batch of cookies, so Hallie put two of them into her sugar sack for Jimmy and his brother. Jimmy had become her friend. Once, after Mrs. Powell held up her history test and announced Hallie had gotten a hundred on it, a boy had said, "Smarty-pants."

"Aw, shut up," Jimmy had told him. "She's all right." Mrs. Powell smiled at that.

Jimmy wasn't in school now, and Hallie wondered why.

She hadn't seen him for a week. "Where's Jimmy? Is he sick?" she asked Cathy.

"He quit."

"Quit! Why?" Hallie was stunned. Jimmy was only a few months away from graduating from eighth grade.

"His dad made him quit. He said Jimmy needed to get a job to help support his family."

"But it's winter. Who hires in winter? Who hires the rest of the year, for that matter?"

Cathy shrugged. "His father doesn't care about school."

Hallie felt bad about Jimmy. She told him so one afternoon when she ran into him at the gas station. He was asking Mr. Ulman about a job, but the man had said he wasn't hiring.

"I'm sorry you had to leave school," Hallie said.

Jimmy shrugged. His shoulders slumped, he started to walk away.

"I could help you," she said suddenly. "I can't go to school every day because I have to take care of my brother. Mrs. Powell gives me lessons ahead of time. You could ask her for your lessons, and I'll help you with them. We can go over them together. I bet if we did that, you could graduate."

Jimmy stared at her. Then he shook his head. "You don't

get it, Hallie. Pa doesn't care if I finish school. He thinks school is a waste of time."

⁓

The Turners found the winter especially hard. Hallie worried about where money would come from. Mr. Carlson didn't need Tom's help anymore. He said he was sorry. He knew Tom needed the money, but he couldn't afford to pay him for doing nothing. Tom went around to the other farms, hoping he'd have better luck. He didn't.

"I'd like to hire you. Swede Carlson put in a good word for you," one farmer told him. "Things are hard for me, too. I can't even pay myself."

Work slacked off at the garage. Since it was winter, the farmers weren't bringing in their machinery to be repaired. Often when Tom went to work, Mr. Ulman told him he wasn't needed that day.

The Turners weren't going hungry, but their meals were lighter. Sometimes they ate only pancakes or bean soup or corn bread with sorghum molasses for supper. From time to time, Mr. Carlson gave them a ham from the smokehouse or Mrs. Carlson sent loaves of bread. There were only a few scoops of sugar left in the sugar sack, but Hallie wouldn't spend their dwindling cash for another bag of it. She wondered sometimes if for Benny's sake, they should have moved in with the Carlsons. But the decision had been the right one. Perhaps the Carlsons thought so, too. They were friendly and generous, but they didn't interfere. They let Tom and Hallie live their own lives.

"No beans. Cake," Benny said one evening when Hallie served bean soup for the third day in a row.

"I'm sorry, Benny. There's no cake," she said.

"No more beans," he told her.

That afternoon, Hallie had searched the woods for ferns or even young thistles that they could eat. It was still winter and too early for them. She gave Benny the choice of bean soup again or pancakes.

The little money Tom earned at the garage now went for food. There was nothing left over for anything else. Hallie no longer bought kerosene for the lamp. She was frugal with what was left of the kerosene, and the Turners went to bed when it grew dark. There was no money for shoes, either. Hallie's shoes pinched her toes, and the soles had so many holes in them that she had to replace the cardboard inserts every few days. She was always on the lookout for discarded cardboard.

"Maybe we should have gone to California after all," Hallie said one night. She had opened the purse where they kept their money and spread it on the table. There were nickels and dimes and pennies but only a single dollar bill. "We don't have any more money now than when we came."

"We might have, if we'd moved in with the Carlsons," Tom shot back at her. He softened. "At least in Kansas we have a place to live."

"I like Kansas," Benny said.

"So do I," Tom agreed. "I like it pretty well, but I've got to find more work."

"At least you've got a job at the garage," Hallie said.

Harold seemed to use any excuse to torment the Turners.

A few people had begun to accept them, but not Harold. One day, outside the filling station, Harold aimed his car at Benny, then swerved at the last minute.

"Bad boy," Benny called.

Harold pulled to a stop. "Who you calling bad boy?" he asked.

"You!" Benny shouted.

"You're that stupid kid."

"Don't say 'stupid.'"

"Stupid, stupid, stupid."

"Stop!" Benny cried, covering his ears.

"Forget it, Harold. Stop picking on the kid," Dan said.

Benny had been by himself outside the filling station. Hallie heard the yelling and rushed out of the office to Benny's side. "What's wrong?" she asked her brother. She glared at Harold.

"He said 'stupid,'" Benny told her.

"He's just talking about himself."

"You can't say that." Harold opened the car door and started toward Hallie.

"Hey," Tom said. He'd been working on a car. He came out of the garage, wiping his hands on a rag. He looked from

Hallie to Harold. "Keep away from her!"

"You think you can stop me?"

"If I have to." Tom made a fist with his right hand.

"Don't, Tom. I'm all right," Hallie told him.

Tom lowered his hand. "You're right. He's just a creep."

"You can't call me a creep," Harold yelled. He spun around and hit Tom in the face.

Tom glared at him but didn't hit back.

"What's the matter? You a coward?" Harold yelled.

"I don't want to fight you," Tom said.

"Seems like you don't have a choice," Harold told him. He moved in and began hitting Tom.

Tom tried to protect himself, but Harold was right. He didn't have a choice. Tom struck out and landed a punch that sent Harold sprawling.

"You broke my nose, you dumb squatter," Harold said, starting to get back up.

A woman called out, "Stop it! Stop it right now."

Hallie had been clutching Benny, who was terrified. She now turned to see Mrs. Powell standing with a group of people. They'd seen the fight.

"He started it," Harold said, getting to his feet. "I was

just defending myself."

"No such thing. I saw you hit him first," the teacher said. "Now you boys shake hands."

Tom slowly held out his hand.

Harold stared at Tom, until Dan said, "Come on and shake. It won't hurt you."

"Shut up," Harold told him, and he walked away from Tom. He got back into the car, then turned and called out, "You won't get away with this."

"Come on, let's go," Dan said. Harold sneered at Tom, then started the engine and drove off.

"I hope that's the end of it," Hallie said as she brushed dirt off Tom.

"I wouldn't count on it," Tom told her.

Hallie knew he was right.

A few days later, Tom was working at the garage when Harold and Dan drove in for gasoline. Mr. Ulman was working on a car. He told Tom to pump the gas into Harold's automobile. "Be careful. I hear those boys are on the warpath," he said.

Tom glanced at Hallie, who was sitting on a bench in front of the station. She had stopped on her way from school to walk home with Tom. Harold, Dan beside him, ignored her. In fact, Hallie wondered if they'd even noticed her. She stared at the car. One fender was smashed, a headlight was gone, and there were scratches on the doors. The car was covered with dirt and grime, too. *You're not much of a driver,* she thought.

"Hey, boy, see if you can fill the tank without spilling the gas," Harold called.

Tom didn't reply. He removed the gas cap and took down the hose and stood beside the car while the gasoline splashed into the tank. When the tank was full, Tom replaced the gas cap and hose. He washed the car windows. Then he went to the driver's side of the Terraplane and said, "That'll be seventy-six cents."

Harold pulled out his billfold and handed Tom a bill. "Don't forget the change," he called after Tom.

When Tom went inside to the cash drawer, Hallie overheard Harold tell Dan, "Watch this. I'll get that dumb squatter."

Tom returned and counted out two dimes and four

pennies. "Here's your change," he said, handing it to Harold.

Harold looked at the money. "Like heck it is!" he said. "I gave you a five-dollar bill. Where's the rest of it?"

"You gave me a dollar."

"You trying to cheat me?"

"No, sir."

Hallie winced, hearing Tom call Harold "sir."

"Then go back and get the rest of my money."

"You gave me a dollar."

"You better go inside and check. I gave you a fiver."

Tom swallowed hard and went back inside to the cash drawer. When he returned, he said, "There's no five-dollar bill in there."

"Hey, Mr. Ulman," Harold called. "Your boy here shorted me four dollars."

Mr. Ulman pushed himself out from under a car and stood. He wiped his greasy hands on his overalls. "What's the problem here?" he asked.

"I gave that squatter a fiver. He said it was a one. He owes me four dollars."

Mr. Ulman turned to Tom. "Is that right?"

"No, sir. I went back and checked. There's no five-dollar

bill in the cash drawer."

"Then he must have put it in his pocket. Turn out your pockets, boy," Harold said.

Mr. Ulman held up his hand to Tom. "No need for that." He stared at the two boys in the car for a long time. "If Tom here says you gave him a one, then you gave him a one. I believe him. Now you boys go on about your business and stop trying to cause trouble."

"He's the one causing the trouble. This isn't the end of it," Harold said, starting the car. He drove off at a high speed, barely missing a dog in the middle of the road.

Mr. Ulman watched them go. "That Harold is a trouble-maker. You watch yourself. They're up to no good."

Thirty minutes later, Hallie helped Tom and Mr. Ulman close up the station. She drew the shades and turned around the "Open" sign so that it read "Closed."

Just as Mr. Ulman was locking the door, Harold drove up and screeched to a stop. Dan wasn't with him. Instead, a man Hallie thought must be Harold's father sat in the passenger seat. He didn't get out of the car but motioned for Mr. Ulman to come over to him. "What can I do for you, Mr. Morton?" Mr. Ulman asked.

"I hear you got a thief working for you," Mr. Morton said.

"No, sir. Tom here is an honest man."

"Not from what my son tells me. He believes the boy owes him four dollars."

"No, sir. Your son gave him a dollar bill. There's no five in the cash drawer."

"Then it looks like the boy pocketed the money."

"He wouldn't do that, Mr. Morton. He's as honest as any young man that's ever worked for me."

"Are you calling my son a liar?"

"I'm saying he made a mistake. But if you believe I owe him four dollars, I'll give it to him." Mr. Ulman took a key out of his pocket and started for the door.

"Now hold on there, Ulman. That's not good enough. It's not just the four dollars. I wouldn't want to do business with a man that employs a thief."

Mr. Ulman stopped and stared. "What's that mean?"

"It seems to me you're a little behind on your loan."

Hallie remembered then that Mr. Morton owned the bank. He must have loaned money to Mr. Ulman for the gas station. Maybe Mr. Ulman had missed a payment. Maybe he'd missed more than one payment.

Mr. Ulman waited.

"I've been understanding about that loan. But if you insist on employing undesirables like that boy over there, well, maybe I'll just reconsider how understanding I've been. I sure would hate to shut you down, but it's the principle of the thing."

"You mean . . . ?" Mr. Ulman asked.

"It's not good business to loan money to a man who employs a thief."

"Tom's not . . ." Mr. Ulman looked down at his hands.

"Think it over, and let me know in the morning. Good day," Mr. Morton said. He nodded at Harold, who grinned at Tom as he revved the engine. The car sped off.

Hallie, Tom, and Mr. Ulman watched the car until it disappeared. Then Mr. Ulman turned to Tom. "I don't have the money to pay the bank. And I have a family that's got to eat. If I lose the garage, I won't be any better off than you are." He shook his head and turned away from Tom, embarrassed to look at him.

"I understand," Tom said.

"I'm real sorry, son. You've been the best mechanic I ever

had. If there was any other way." He punched his right fist into the palm of his left hand.

"It's all right," Tom said. "We'll make out."

Tom and Hallie started off down the road, but Mr. Ulman called for Tom to wait a minute. He went inside and came out with six one-dollar bills in his hand. "Here's two weeks' pay. It's the least I can do."

Hallie felt Tom stiffen. She knew he wanted to turn down the money even though they needed it. He didn't want to take a handout.

Mr. Ulman must have realized that, too. He said, "Heck, I was going to give four dollars to Harold just so's you could stay on. You might as well take it instead."

Tom relented and put out his hand. "I sure do thank you, Mr. Ulman."

"If I hear of anything, I'll let you know." Mr. Ulman shook his head again. "Those boys are a worthless pair. They may not be done with you yet. You be careful."

~

"I let you down," Tom told Hallie as they walked along the

road toward the Carlson farm to get Benny.

"You didn't let us down. You've been carrying the load ever since we left Oklahoma," Hallie told him. "You must feel the way Daddy did when he left us."

"I won't leave you."

"I know that."

"How are we going to live?"

"We haven't starved yet."

"Some people sure don't like us much." Tom walked slowly, his shoulders slumped, kicking rocks in the road. "Maybe you were right when you said we should move on. Maybe we should do that now."

"Maybe," Hallie said. "But we don't have the money for gas to go anywhere far."

They walked along silently for a moment. Then Hallie said, "I'm proud of you, Tom. You did the right thing. You can't give up. Remember when Daddy left and never came back? Mommy said the measure of a man was how he stood up to bad times. I'm not sure exactly what that means, but I think she was saying that you can tell what a person's made of by how he deals with trouble. You could have gone off, too, but you didn't. Mommy knew you wouldn't. I did, too. That's the difference between you and Daddy. You face trouble, and you don't give up."

"You don't give up, either, Hallie."

"I'm tempted to sometimes."

Tom kicked hard at a rock that skittered off into the ditch. "We aren't neither one of us giving up, I reckon."

"We make a pretty good team," Hallie told him.

"You and me." Tom smiled a little at her.

"And Benny," Hallie said.

"And Benny."

The two stopped at the Carlsons' to collect the little boy. Just as they were leaving, Mr. Carlson said, "I was about to take my old truck to the station so's you could look at it. It don't start too good."

"Mr. Ulman'll be glad to fix it," Tom said.

"I was hoping you'd fix it."

Tom looked off into the distance. "I don't work there anymore, Mr. Carlson."

"You quit him? I thought you liked working there."

"I surely did. I didn't quit."

"Mr. Ulman had to let him go on account of Mr. Morton threatened him," Hallie said. "Harold Morton claimed Tom stole four dollars from him."

Mr. Carlson's face dropped. "I don't believe for a minute you'd do a thing like that."

"Mr. Ulman doesn't, either," Hallie said. "But he didn't have a choice."

"Why, anybody who knows you, Tom, would take your word over Harold's," Mrs. Carlson said.

"Anybody but Mr. Morton," Hallie said.

"I suppose you're right about that." Mr. Carlson exchanged a glance with his wife. Then he cleared his throat. "It's almost spring, and I was thinking of starting planting a little early this year, maybe next month. Fields has got to be ready in case it rains."

Tom looked up quickly. "Rain?"

"Well, you never know. We had rain two, three years ago. I'm hoping I'll see it again before I die. Might say it's a dream of mine. Could be it'll rain this year. You be available to help me?"

"Yes, sir," Tom said. "Thank you, Mr. Carlson."

"Can you hold out till then?"

"You bet," Hallie said, crossing her fingers for luck.

chapter twelve

More Trouble

"That must be Mr. Carlson," Hallie said one day in mid-March. She'd heard a car pull up and stop near the cabin. They had just finished eating supper. Mrs. Carlson had given them a chicken a few days before. They had already eaten the chicken, so that day Hallie had added the bones to the bean soup, creating a rich broth.

"Doesn't sound like Mr. Carlson's car," Tom said. "I'll go see who it is."

He opened the door, and he and Hallie stared at a big black car parked in the yard. A man sat behind the wheel. In farm country, a stranger didn't just go to the door and knock. He waited for someone to come out of the house. Tom went down the steps and stood in the yard. Hallie remained in the doorway. The man turned off the engine and opened the car door. He was a big man, and he had to swivel around on the seat to get out.

"You Tom Turner?" the man asked.

"I am."

Hallie stepped down beside Tom. Something about the man frightened her. He had a sense of authority. She knew he was someone important. He wasn't a farmer looking for workers.

"I'm Sheriff Eagles," the man said.

"Thought you might be," Tom said.

The man frowned. "Why's that?"

"The badge pinned to your coat."

The sheriff glanced down at the badge and smiled. "Guess that'd be a hint, all right."

Tom didn't invite him in. Instead, he asked, "What can we do for you, sir?"

"I come to talk to you."

"Maybe he's looking for a good farmhand," Hallie whispered.

The sheriff heard her. "Don't have a farm."

"We got coffee," Hallie said suddenly. "You want a cup?"

The sheriff smiled then and took off his hat. "I sure would, if it wouldn't rob you, Miss Turner."

"You come right inside," she told him. Mommy had said you got more flies with sorghum than with vinegar. If the sheriff was there because of what had happened at the filling station, they ought to be nice to him.

The sheriff stepped inside the cabin and looked around. "You got it awful good here," he said.

"Yes, sir, awful good," Hallie told him. "Thanks to the Carlsons."

"They're fine folks."

Hallie glanced at Tom, who hadn't said a word. He was staring at Sheriff Eagles's badge. Hallie knew the man hadn't just stopped by on a friendly visit. Something was wrong. That was why the sheriff knew Tom's name. She worried that Mr. Morton had complained about the four dollars. Hallie poured the last of their coffee into a tin cup and handed it to the sheriff. "You want sugar?" She hoped not. They had only a little left in the sugar bowl.

"Don't need it. You make a good cup of coffee, Miss

Turner," he said after tasting it.

"You can call me Hallie."

"Miss Hallie."

"I'd give you pie, but we don't have any."

"Times is tough."

"You can say that again." She wished Tom would say something. She'd used up all her conversation.

"Hi, I'm Benny. I have soup," Benny said.

"Hi, yourself, Mr. Benny."

"I'm not *Mr.* Benny." Benny laughed.

Sheriff Eagles pulled a chair from the table and sat down. So did Hallie, but Tom remained standing. "I hear you been working for the Carlsons. They're as good as we got around here."

"Yes, sir," Tom said, speaking at last.

"Carlsons been on that farm for a long time. Carlson's daddy and my daddy, they go way back. Come here when there was still Indians around." He chuckled at that. "The Indians used to come to the house and bother my grandmother, always asking for corn bread." The sheriff shook his head, thinking about that. Then he turned to look directly at Tom. "You been here, what, five, six months now?"

"A little more," Tom said. "This is March. We got here in August."

"You planning on staying?"

Hallie fidgeted in her chair. Maybe the sheriff was going to tell them to move on. She'd heard of lawmen who were hard on outsiders. They destroyed possessions and even beat the migrants sometimes. Maybe she shouldn't have invited Sheriff Eagles into the house.

"Any reason we shouldn't?" Tom asked.

The sheriff shrugged.

"We were headed for California when the car broke down. Right here. We like Kansas right well," Hallie said. "Maybe we'll go on if Tom can't get a job."

"I heard he's a worker." The sheriff finished his coffee and set down his cup. It banged against the table. Hallie thought to ask if he wanted more, but she remembered there wasn't any more. It was time for him to tell them why he was there.

"I've been sheriff here for quite a bit. I've got old doing it." The sheriff was a powerful man, but his hair was white, and his skin was blotchy with age spots. "I ain't as old as I look. I can still catch a thief or two. Not that this town has many of them. There was a fellow came through here once. He tried to steal a kitchen stove. It was one of those gas ones, not like yours." He pointed to the cook stove. "He didn't know you had to unhook the gas. Blew up in his face. Near took the kitchen out of that house." He shook his head. "I guess I could tell you lots of stories, most of them about thieving. Some of them about mischief." He turned and stared at Tom.

Tom stared back.

"What's your business here?" Hallie asked.

"Business? Who says I got business?"

"Is this just a friendly call?" Tom asked.

"Well, I do like to know my neighbors. And seeing as how you've been here better than half the year, you qualify as a neighbor. And you being orphans and all, I guess it's time I check to see how you're getting on. It ain't easy being on your own when you're young like you are, but there ain't enough orphanages to take care of everybody. And from what I hear, they ain't always the best place to live neither. Carlsons look after you, do they?"

Neither Tom nor Hallie answered.

The sheriff turned his chair so that he was looking

directly at Tom, who was still standing. He cleared his throat. "You know the Morton boy, do you? Harold by name."

Tom barely nodded.

"How's that?" the sheriff asked.

"I think you know I do."

"Get along, do you?"

"I expect you know the answer to that, too."

"So I've heard."

Suddenly Tom slammed his hand on the table. "If this is about that four dollars, I didn't take it!"

Startled, Hallie looked at her brother. Benny, frightened, glanced from Tom to the sheriff.

"Four dollars?" the sheriff said.

Hallie wished Tom had kept his mouth shut, but he was too riled up. "That four dollars he says I stole from him."

"Now, why would he say that?"

"Because he's a jerk. Because he doesn't like us. He thinks we're trash."

The sheriff cocked his head to one side. "That right?"

"No, it isn't. We're not trash! We're down on our luck, just like people all over. We're decent folks."

"We're just looking for someplace to call home. We're

not after trouble," Hallie said. "I heard Harold tell Dan he was going to fix Tom. I was sitting right there. They didn't see me," she added.

The sheriff didn't speak.

"You can ask Mr. Ulman about that four dollars. Harold gave me a dollar. When I handed him change, he said he'd given me a five. But he hadn't. I checked the change drawer. Mr. Ulman knew I was right. He had to fire me because of Harold's dad. Mr. Morton said he'd call the loan on the garage if I kept on working there. Ask him."

"I done that."

Tom blinked, not knowing what else to say.

"What did Mr. Ulman tell you?" Hallie asked. Benny had come over to her and laid his head in her lap. He didn't like the angry talk.

"He said the Morton boy was just causing trouble. There's been bad blood between him and Tom ever since you come here, he says." The sheriff leaned forward. "I have to say that Morton kid is so dumb he couldn't count to ten if he used his fingers. So it wouldn't surprise me if he mistook a dollar bill for a five."

"He did it on purpose," Hallie said.

"That wouldn't surprise me neither." The sheriff leaned back in his chair and chuckled. Then he grew serious. "I'm not here about no four dollars. That's not the reason I come."

Hallie and Tom stared at him. They couldn't imagine what had brought the sheriff to the cabin.

"You going to tell us what that reason is?" Tom asked.

"I am." The sheriff stood. He was even bigger than Hallie had thought. It seemed he had swollen in size until he filled up the room. "Harold Morton's car's been stole."

"And you think I took it?" Tom asked.

Hallie pinched her lips together. "Tom did no such thing. He never stole a thing in his life."

"I didn't say he done it."

"Then why are you here?" Tom asked.

"Because I don't know who stole it. Old Morton says it was you. Harold, too, and that tagalong friend of his, Dan. So I got to check it out. But they don't got no proof."

"No, they don't," Hallie said.

"Still, everybody knows Tom don't get along with Harold Morton. That's no secret. If somebody was to steal Harold's car, Tom here would be a good bet."

"Why do you say that?" Hallie asked.

The sheriff held up his hand. "I don't have no proof. That's the truth. But Tom knows all about cars. It wouldn't be hard for him to start the engine without a key." The sheriff nodded to underscore his words. "Maybe he wouldn't even need to do that. The boy always left the key in his car." He thought a moment. "There's those would say whoever stole that automobile maybe did a good turn. It's a surprise he never run anybody over, the way he drives. Last time I saw the car, it was pretty beat-up. He was a menace, all right." He looked at Tom a long time. "Maybe you thought you was protecting the town when you took his car. Maybe you just wanted the borrow of it."

"I didn't take it," Tom said so fiercely that Benny raised his head from Hallie's lap.

"It's okay, Benny," she said, patting his back.

"I don't guess anybody could blame you much, Harold taking your job away. And then that beating Harold give you. Way I heard it, he got the best of you."

"He did not!" Hallie flared. "Tom didn't start it, either. Mrs. Powell from the school saw it. Ask her."

"Yeah," Benny said.

"You saw it, too, did you, son?" the sheriff asked.

Benny looked confused.

"You saw Harold?" the sheriff asked.

"Bad boy," Benny said.

"I wouldn't argue with you there."

"Ask my teacher," Hallie said.

"I already did. She thinks Harold would rather fight dirty and lose than fight fair and win." He put his hat on, then touched the brim to Hallie. "Sis," he said. "See you in church."

"We don't go to church," Tom told him.

"Well, neither do I." He laughed. "But I expect your reason is not because you get up a poker game every Sunday morning like I do."

Despite herself, Hallie smiled.

Sheriff Eagles started for the door. Just as he got there, he turned around as if he'd forgotten something. "There's one other thing, Tom," he said.

Tom stiffened. "What's that?"

"What was you doing outside the Morton house Monday evening this week? That's the day the car was stole."

"I—"

The sheriff raised his hand. "Before you say anything, I

best tell you, you was seen there. It wasn't any of the Mortons told me. Somebody else."

Tom looked away. He didn't speak for a long time. "It's nobody's business."

"You was there, then?"

Hallie went over and stood beside Tom.

"Yes, sir."

"For what reason?"

"Like I say, that's my business."

The sheriff frowned. "Might be we could clear this up if you'd tell me."

"I won't. I was there, but I didn't steal any car."

The sheriff stared at Tom for a long time. Then he stepped through the doorway. "I advise you not to leave the county, not till this is settled. You understand?"

"Yes, sir."

Tom and Hallie stood in the doorway, Hallie holding on to Benny. They watched as the sheriff backed onto the road and took off. Then Tom walked down into the yard and sat on a log in the dark. Hallie came and sat next to him and pulled Benny into her lap. "I don't like him," Benny said.

"It's all right, Benny. He's a good man. He just has a job

to do," Hallie told him.

"Okay," Benny said.

"Don't ask why I was over by the Morton house," Tom told his sister.

"I won't."

Tom thought for a long time. "Maybe we just ought to take out and go to California like you wanted to. Looks like we're not welcome in Kansas anymore."

Hallie took her older brother's hand. "If we leave, people will believe you're guilty. Running away from trouble is not our way. We'll work this out—together."

Hallie's Discovery

*E*veryone knew that Harold's car was gone. And they knew that Harold had accused Tom of stealing it. In fact, that was all anybody talked about the next day at school.

"They're not but squatters. My dad says we should drive them out," one of Wilma's friends said. The other girls stared at Hallie as they nodded in agreement. Wilma didn't nod, but she didn't look at Hallie, either. At recess, when the students chose sides for games, Hallie was the last one picked. After Mrs. Powell announced that Hallie had gotten the top grade with her essay, a girl whispered, "That's because she cheats. She's dishonest, like her brother." Mildred, who sat beside

Hallie in class, moved to another desk. *She'll be sorry*, Hallie thought, smiling to herself. Mildred was about as smart as a doughnut. Whose test answers could she copy now?

Cathy was loyal, however. She stayed by Hallie's side during the dinner break. "Who do you think stole Harold's car?" she asked.

"Probably some tramp. He's all the way to Colorado by now. They'll never find the car. As long as we live here, people will believe Tom's guilty." Hallie remembered her brash talk about not running away from trouble and wondered if she had been right.

Cathy seemed to know what Hallie was thinking. "Why don't you go to California? My mother wanted to go there when we lost our place, but Dad said we had to come to Kansas to help my grandparents on the farm."

"If we left, we'd never be able to hold up our heads again," Hallie replied.

"But in California, nobody would know who you are."

"We would. We'd know we were cowards."

"It doesn't even make sense that your brother would steal it."

"Yeah, what would he do with it, park it behind our

cabin?" Hallie asked sarcastically. "And if he drove it into town, don't you think somebody might notice?"

"Maybe whoever took it drove it to Topeka and sold it."

"That would be dumb. How many cars like that are there in Kansas?"

"Especially one as beat-up as Harold's." Cathy laughed.

Things weren't much different around town. A woman at the mercantile clutched her pocketbook when she saw Hallie standing next to her. Did she think that because she believed Tom had stolen the car, Hallie was not to be trusted around the woman's purse? A man who had promised Tom work in the spring sent his son to say Tom wouldn't be needed after all.

To her surprise, however, Hallie discovered that not everybody was against them. A farmer stopped one morning at the cabin and asked Tom if he'd come by and take a look at a truck he had that wouldn't start. A woman told Hallie she'd seen the apron Hallie had made for Mrs. Carlson at Christmas and asked if she would make two for her, for gifts. She'd provide the material and would pay Hallie fifty cents for each apron for her labor. Others said they knew Tom hadn't stolen any car. They said they believed him.

One afternoon the minister came to the cabin with a batch of cookies his wife had baked. "She thought the little boy might like them," he said, handing a sugar sack to Benny. "I should have called on you before this, but I've been laid up. You'll excuse me for not being neighborly."

Hallie wasn't quite sure why he'd stopped. Did he expect Tom to confess and ask for forgiveness?

The minister didn't say a word about the stolen car. He asked Benny how high he could count and whether he knew how to spell his name. Then he asked Benny to sing "Happy Days." Benny's voice was off-key. He scrambled the words, but he beamed when he was finished.

"I couldn't have sung it better myself," the minister said. He told Tom he wished he had work for him at the church. The collection was barely enough to pay his salary, however. Besides, the congregation expected *him* to keep the building in good repair. Then he said to Hallie, "My sister says you're a bright girl."

"Your sister?" Hallie asked.

"Mrs. Powell." He'd taken off his hat when he

approached the cabin. Now he put it back on. Hallie thought he'd want to pray over them before he left, but the minister didn't say anything about that. "I sure am glad I had a chance to get to know you folks," he told them.

Just as he was leaving, Sheriff Eagles pulled his big car up to the cabin.

"Sheriff," the minister said.

"Reverend."

They watched as the minister got into a car almost as old as the Turners' Model T and drove off.

"If I went to church, I'd go to his," the sheriff said. "If I went to church."

"He's nice," Benny said. He'd eaten one cookie and held another in his hand.

"Yes, sir, Mr. Benny," the sheriff said. Benny laughed.

Hallie laughed, too, but Tom only glared at the sheriff. "You still think I stole that car?"

"I don't know who stole it. You got any idea?"

"Why ask me?"

"You might know of somebody who'd do mischief. You aren't the only one those two boys were out to get."

"Then ask them. I think somebody passing through stole

it. Otherwise, we'd have seen it around town."

"Who'd be fool enough to drive a stolen Terraplane around here?"

"Only one I know that foolish is Harold Morton," Hallie said.

"You got that right, Miss Hallie." The sheriff chuckled. "By the way, his daddy already ordered him another car. Should be here in a week."

"Wonder how long before it's beat-up," Tom said. "That Terraplane was a swell car, but Harold didn't treat it right." Tom smiled a little. "He didn't know you had to add oil. He almost burned out the engine."

"Well, you let me know if you get any bright ideas. Thing is, we got the word out all over Kansas, and nobody's seen a roughed-up Terraplane. That means it might be hid somewheres."

Tom clenched his fists. "Are you saying I hid it? Well, you just look around. Look in the cabin, for all I care. Look in the Carlsons' barn. You think Mr. Carlson would let me hide it there?"

Sheriff Eagles held up his hands. "Now don't get all riled up, boy. Truth is, I don't think you had anything to do with it. But you got to admit that you being over by the Mortons' the night it was stole is awful suspicious. I sure wish you'd tell me what that was about."

"It's not your business," Tom said.

"Tom—" Hallie said.

"Be still," Tom told her, and he went inside the house, leaving Hallie and the sheriff watching him.

"Sis, if you know something . . . ," Sheriff Eagles said.

Hallie shook her head. "I don't know anything." *But I can guess.*

Harold's car had been gone almost a week when Hallie decided to look for spring dandelion greens. The weather had suddenly turned warm, and dandelions were springing up all over. Tom had taken Benny to the Carlsons, so Hallie went alone. She thought Benny would love the leaves cooked with a little bacon grease.

She searched along the road north of the cabin, stepping off into grassy areas when she spotted clusters of bright yellow dandelion flowers. She was careful to collect only the young leaves. The big dark green ones were tough and bitter. There were plenty of dandelions, and her sugar sack was almost full. There was room for only a few more.

Hallie reached for a clump of pale green leaves, then stopped and said, "Ugh." In the middle of the plant was a cigarette butt, a ready-made. Plenty of men smoked. Hallie had seen them throw the butts out of the car windows as they passed. Most men rolled their own cigarettes, of course. Who could afford ready-mades? The butt was a long way from the road, and she wondered who could throw a cigarette that far. Maybe a tramp had been walking through the woods, but tramps didn't smoke ready-mades.

The dandelions had popped up in the middle of a tire track. Hallie could make out the treads of the tires in the dirt. *That's odd*, she thought. There wasn't a house nearby. So there was no reason for a car to turn off. Why would someone drive a car into the woods? Curious, she followed the tracks. She set down her sugar sack of greens and slowly walked along the treads into a dense collection of bushes and trees. The bushes were broken, as if a car had been driven over them.

Hallie walked past them until she saw a gleam of metal.

Then she pushed the bushes aside and found herself looking at a car—a Terraplane. Harold's Terraplane. She stood and stared. It was Harold's car, all right, but it was in worse shape than ever. The driver's door was bashed in. Hallie made her way through the underbrush to the front of the car. The grill was broken and the front window smashed. That couldn't have happened when the car went off the road into the brush. The car must have been in an accident before that. Whoever had stolen it must have first crashed the car, then abandoned it.

Hallie went back for her sack of greens and started for home. She would tell Tom what she'd found. But as she walked back down the road, she changed her mind. Her brother would want to see that car. She worried if the sheriff saw their footprints around it, he might say Tom had stolen it. After all, how could you tell if footprints were made that day or a week before? She walked past the turnoff to the cabin and hurried on.

The sheriff's office was on the near side of town. Hallie had been by it a dozen times, but she'd never been inside. There had been no reason to go in. With the iron bars on the windows, the place looked scary, and she always walked quickly past it on her way to school.

Now she pushed open the door and stood a moment, letting her eyes adjust. The office was dark, and it took her a moment to see the inside. There was a potbellied stove in the center with a long stovepipe going through the roof. The jail cells were visible through a back door. A wooden desk was in the center of the room. A stack of papers was piled so high on it that it almost blocked out the sheriff, who sat in a chair at the desk. He'd been reading, and now he looked up at Hallie, tilting his head so that he could see her through his spectacles.

"Well, hello there. What can I do for you?" he asked. Then he recognized her and smiled. "You're Miss Hallie Turner. Am I right?"

"Yes, sir."

"You bring me a sack of greens, did you?"

She had forgotten she was holding the sugar sack and put it behind her back. "No, sir."

He waited, but Hallie said nothing. She couldn't think how to tell him what she'd found. Maybe coming there was a mistake. After all, she was Tom's sister. If she told the sheriff about the car, he'd think for sure that Tom had stolen it.

Maybe he'd even think she had helped Tom hide it and that the two of them had come up with the idea of her pretending to find it.

The sheriff removed some papers from a chair beside his desk and patted the seat. "Why don't you sit right here and tell me why you come?"

"I . . ." Hallie wondered if she should just leave. She could say she'd gotten the wrong building, that she was looking for the post office. But the sheriff would know better. Everybody knew where the post office was.

"Is it about your brother?"

Hallie looked down at her feet. Slowly she walked to the chair and sat down.

The sheriff opened a desk drawer and took out a package of gum and handed it to her. Hallie took a stick, but instead of unwrapping it, she put it into the sugar sack. She would save it for Benny.

"Well, sis?"

"I found the car." Her voice was so low that she could hardly hear herself.

"How's that?" The sheriff leaned toward her. He used his right forefinger to push his ear forward.

"I found the car."

"The car?"

"Harold's car. The one that got stolen."

"That so?"

Hallie wished he'd say something more to make it easier for her, but he didn't.

"It's off the road. In the bushes."

"Near your place?"

"Up the road." Hallie realized how bad that sounded. "Way up the road."

"But not too far."

"No."

"Makes sense."

Hallie had put the sack of greens on her lap. Now she gripped the edges of the bag in her fists. "I was collecting dandelion greens. I saw a cigarette butt on the ground. And then I saw tire marks. So I followed them. The car's all smashed up. Whoever stole it wrecked it first."

"I guess that's no surprise," Sheriff Eagles muttered. He stood up. "Well, sis, I guess you better show me where it's at."

Hallie slumped in the chair. "Do I have to? Can't I just tell you?"

"No, you come along. We'll take my car. I'll drop you off at home when I'm done. I'll want to talk to your brother."

"He didn't steal it!"

Sheriff Eagles smiled. "So he says. He's got some questions to answer. I'd like to know what he was up to over at the Morton place that night."

"I can't tell you."

"You know?"

Hallie realized she shouldn't have spoken. "I don't know for sure."

The sheriff didn't push her. Instead, he yelled through the back door, "Don't you make any trouble back there. I'll be around in time for your supper. Won't do you any harm to wait."

Hallie shivered and tried to see through the door. "Do you have somebody bad locked up in there?"

"Just a hobo. He was drunk. He needed a place to sleep it off. I'll send him on his way tomorrow." He led Hallie outside and opened the front passenger door of his car for her.

The car had a big star on the side. Hallie slunk down in the seat for fear somebody would see her and think she'd been arrested. She waited until the car was out of town before she sat up straight. They passed the turnoff to the cabin, and Sheriff Eagles slowed down.

"There," Hallie said. "See those tracks. That's where somebody drove off the road."

"This the first time you seen 'em?"

"I don't go up that way much. The Carlson place is between us and town. I just thought it was a good place to look for dandelions."

Sheriff Eagles pulled over and turned off the engine. Hallie got out of the car and started through the brush. The sheriff told her to wait while he looked around. He searched the ground and spotted the cigarette butt Hallie pointed out to him. He picked it up and put it into his pocket.

Then he walked back and forth, studying the ground, occasionally leaning over to pick up something. He pulled threads off a bush and put them into his pocket. Finally he reached the wrecked car. "You didn't touch anything, did you, sis?" he asked.

"No, sir."

"Good."

The driver's-side door was unlocked, and the sheriff put his handkerchief over the car handle to pull it wide so that he could look inside. He reached for a jacket that was on the floor by the passenger seat. "You ever seen this?" he asked.

Hallie gasped. "It's Tom's," she said, quickly covering her mouth with her hand. She shouldn't have told the sheriff. She shouldn't have told him about the car, either. She was getting Tom into more and more trouble. Hallie added quickly, "He lost it in the winter. Or somebody took it. I bought him a new one for Christmas. I wouldn't have bought it if he still had the old one."

"Looks like it's been used as a rag." The sheriff dropped it onto the car seat. He looked over the car, careful not to use his bare hand to touch the door handles or the steering wheel. Then he backed out of the vehicle.

"Do you still think Tom stole it?" Hallie asked. She knew she shouldn't ask, but she wanted to warn Tom.

"Do you?"

"I never thought he did."

"I'd feel a whole lot better about him if I knowed why he was hanging around the Morton house that night. You wouldn't want to tell me about that, would you?"

Hallie looked away.

"You want to share that with me?"

"I can't."

"Why's that?" The sheriff sat down on a log near the car and took out a pouch of tobacco. He removed a cigarette paper and spread tobacco on it, then he rolled it together and licked the seam. "You can't tell me even to help out your brother?" He took out a match and struck it on the side of the car, then lit the cigarette.

"We'd be shamed."

"Shame worse than having me think your brother stole the car?" The sheriff spotted another used cigarette on the ground and reached for it. He put it into his pocket. *That makes six or eight cigarettes*, Hallie thought.

She considered the sheriff's words. "If I tell you, can it be a secret? Will you promise you won't tell?"

"Cross my heart."

Hallie looked at the ground. "I think it was the shoes."

"How's that?"

"The shoes. My shoes are so bad that I have to put cardboard in them all the time. And they pinch my feet. I go barefoot most of the time." She glanced down at her feet. "I need new shoes, but we don't have the money. Tom feels bad about that. He says he's let me down." She quickly went on.

"It's not his fault. We just don't have the money."

The sheriff waited.

"You see, there was a pair of women's shoes in the Mortons' trash. I saw them when we were in town. Tom did, too. When he went out after dark that night, I wondered if he was going to get them. But I think somebody else got there first and took the shoes, because Tom didn't bring them home."

"What's so bad about that that you couldn't tell me?"

"Like I said, if anybody knew, we'd be shamed. Tom feels awful bad he lost that job at the garage and that things are so poorly for us. He thinks it's his fault he can't bring in any money. If folks knew he had to go through their trash looking for shoes, well, he wouldn't be able to hold up his head. He's proud, Tom is." Hallie stared at the ground while she talked. When she looked up, her face was red. "You won't tell, will you? You promised. Tom would be awful mad."

"Sounds sensible to me. I gave you my word, sis. You sure that's where he was at?"

Hallie nodded. "After he got home that night, he picked up my shoes and said he sure did wish we had the money for new ones."

The sheriff ground out his cigarette and stood. He picked up Tom's jacket. "I'll drop you off at home."

"Are you going to talk to Tom?"

"I don't need to. You already answered my question."

———

Later that day, Mr. Ulman came down the road in his truck, driving past the cabin. When he came back, he had the Terraplane chained to the back of his truck. Tom and Hallie stood in the yard and watched the truck go by, hauling the car toward town. "I wonder what happened," Tom said.

Hallie didn't reply. The two were discouraged and paid little attention to Benny as he chattered through supper. Hallie was sorry then that she'd told the sheriff about the car. Maybe it would have rotted away and people eventually would have forgotten about it.

Just as they were finishing their pancakes, Sheriff Eagles's car pulled into the yard. The man sat in the vehicle until Tom and Hallie went outside. "I'd like to speak to you folks," the sheriff said.

"You come to arrest me?" Tom asked.

"Like I said, I come to talk."

"We saw Mr. Ulman take the Terraplane down the road. We know it was found," Tom said.

"Didn't Hallie tell you? She's the one who found it."

Tom looked surprised, but Hallie looked away, not saying anything. She hadn't told Tom.

"You might as well come inside," Tom told him.

"We got enough for another hotcake if you want one," Hallie said. She could add a little more water to the batter to stretch it.

The sheriff held up his hand. "I expect my missus is waiting dinner. I got to get on home. But I wanted to stop here first."

Tom and Hallie waited.

"You don't have a cigarette, do you?"

Tom shook his head. "I don't smoke them, even hand rolled."

"That's what I thought. You see there was cigarette butts all around that car. Sis here spotted the first one. There's not many folks around here that smoke ready-mades. And these were some fancy brand. Only person I know who smokes them is Mr. Morton. And I guess young Harold does, too. It seemed right strange to me that there was so many around there, like somebody sat there a long time thinking about what he'd say about that car."

"You mean—?" Tom started to ask, but the sheriff raised his hand again.

"Now, Harold Morton's a hard one, and his father thinks the sun rises and sets on that boy. So I got to thinking about that friend of his—Dan. He isn't a bad sort when he's not around Harold. I went to his place and talked to him. I said we'd found all those cigarettes out there, and there were plenty of fingerprints on the steering wheel. I didn't tell him the county wouldn't pay to have them checked out. I just sort of let him think I done that already. Then I asked if he had anything to tell me."

"Did he?" Hallie asked.

"Did he!" the sheriff answered. "Why, he confessed faster than a fox in a henhouse. He said Harold ran that car into a tree and knew his father would just about kill him for it. So they cooked up that story about the car being stole. Harold had taken Tom's jacket last fall. They left it under the seat so if anybody found the car, they'd think Tom here had stole it. Then they ran it off the road near your place so when it was found, folks would think you hid it nearby. Darndest thing. If Hallie hadn't spotted that cigarette, I never would have proved those boys did it."

"Did Harold confess?" Tom asked.

"Well, not at first. But when I told him Dan admitted what they did and said we had him dead to rights with the fingerprints and the cigarettes, he finally came around. Said they did it as a joke."

"A joke?" Tom said.

"Mr. Morton didn't think it was no joke neither. He said he was sending back Harold's new car. He told Harold he could walk from then on—walk all the way to Topeka, for all he cared."

"Did you arrest them?" Hallie asked. "Will they go to jail?" She smiled at the idea of Harold and Dan sitting in the cell where the tramp had been.

The sheriff put his foot on the running board of his car and shook his head. "I wish I could lock them up. Seems there's no law against running your car into a tree. Or stealing your own car neither. I guess it's up to Mr. Morton to punish Harold."

"What about Tom?" Hallie asked.

"I never did think he stole it. But I didn't have no idea who did."

"I mean, Tom's reputation's ruined. Don't those boys have to pay for that?"

The sheriff shook his head. "Not that I know of. But it will get around. Folks will know Tom's all right."

"Won't Dan and Harold even have to apologize to him?" Hallie asked.

"You'd think they would, but don't hold your breath."

We're not thieves anymore, Hallie thought. *But they still think we're squatters.*

The sheriff tipped his hat to her and started to get into his car. Then he turned around. "Wouldn't surprise me none, Tom, if Ulman offered you your job back. I can't think as how old Morton would object."

chapter fourteen

Benny

Maybe Tom had been right. *Maybe we should go on to California*, Hallie thought. *People are never going to accept us.* Of course, there were good things about Kansas. She loved the little cabin, and the Carlsons had been wonderful. Mrs. Powell and Sheriff Eagles had stood up for them. Mr. Ulman had asked Tom to go back to work at the garage and had even given him a five-cent raise. Mr. Carlson had started spring plowing, and Tom had all the work there that he wanted. On his first payday Tom had bought Hallie new shoes.

Still, Harold and Dan did not apologize. Nor did Mr.

Morton. Things had returned to normal at the school, although nobody told Hallie they were sorry they'd thought her brother was a thief. At recess, when the students chose sides for baseball, Hallie was once again the first girl picked. She hit a home run, but Cathy was the only one who congratulated her. Mildred returned to her old seat next to Hallie, but now Hallie covered up her answers to test questions.

The spring was beautiful in Kansas. Despite the lack of rain, wildflowers sprang up, and Benny picked bouquets of them every time he walked to the Carlson house. The days were sunny and not too hot. Green things popped up in the fields, and there was the scent of freshly turned earth. Eggs hatched. At the Carlson farm, Tessie and Benny played with tiny yellow puffballs of baby chicks, and Mrs. Carlson promised to give Hallie some of them when they were a little older. Mr. Carlson hauled an old chicken coop to the cabin, and Hallie cleaned and repaired it. She knew the chickens were the Carlsons' way of telling the Turners that they were welcome to stay on, at least for a little while. She appreciated that, but still, she wondered if anybody else wanted them there. "Will we always be thought of as squatters?" she asked Tom.

"We're doing all right," he replied. After the sheriff discovered Harold had hid his own car and lied, Tom hadn't said much more about California.

—⁓—

Because it was spring, Hallie decided it was a good time to clean the cabin. She scrubbed the walls and the fireplace. She cleaned and blackened the cook stove until it looked almost new. Then she gathered up the quilts to be laundered. She hauled water from the creek, heated it on the cook stove, and poured it into the big tin tub that she had found hanging on the outside wall of the cabin. The old quilts went into the tub first. She scrubbed them with soap, changing the water twice because they were so dirty.

"I'll help!" Benny had cried as Hallie lifted the first soaked quilt from the rinse water. He picked up one end and Hallie the other.

"We have to twist it to get out the water," Hallie said. Benny laughed as the water drained out of the quilt onto his feet. He helped his sister spread the quilt over the bushes to dry.

Then Hallie took down Mommy's Irish Chain quilt that had been hanging on the wall. It was dirty, too, from smoke that escaped from the stove.

Hallie washed it carefully, making a note of rips or where the tiny squares had pulled loose. She would need to repair the quilt after it dried. She remembered when Mommy had made it. Hallie hadn't known how to quilt then. She had helped her mother by going through the ragbag, searching for pieces of blue material. Mommy had traded scraps with her friends to get additional blue.

"Someday I'll pass this on to you," Mommy had said. And so she had, although Hallie wished Mommy were still there to enjoy it. As she looked at the quilt, she missed Mommy and Barbara and even Daddy. She wondered if they'd ever have a home like the one in Oklahoma again, a home where women sat and sewed, where neighbors dropped in and helped each other out. Maybe there was such a place in California.

She looked around for Benny to help her wring out the Irish Chain quilt. He had been playing in the yard with his blocks, reciting the letters. Then she had heard him call, "Hi, Bob." She hadn't seen him in a while.

"Benny, come help," Hallie called. When he didn't answer, she wrung out the quilt herself and hung it over a tree branch to dry. She thought Benny would like to play under the dripping quilt and yelled, "Come on! It's raining under the quilt." She picked up the laundry tub and poured the rinse water over flowers that she had planted beside the cabin.

Benny didn't answer. *He probably wandered away after Bob,* Hallie thought. He'd done that before. The rabbits were fast, however, so Benny followed them for only a few steps. Hallie called again and went into the woods near the cabin. "Benny!" she yelled. Sometimes the little boy hid, and she wondered if he was hiding now. When there was no answer, Hallie grew concerned. "Benny, come for dinner," she called. Benny was always ready to eat. He didn't reply. Hallie went farther into the woods, but there was no sign of her little brother. She called until she was hoarse. Benny didn't answer. She came back to the creek and followed it. Benny loved water. The creek was shallow. Still, Benny could have fallen and hit his head. Hallie followed the water for a little way. *Benny couldn't have gone that far,* she thought and retraced her steps.

A rabbit darted in front of her and made her think of

Bob. "Bob's here, Benny!" she yelled as loud as she could. He'd come running if he thought Bob was around. Hallie heard a rustling in the brush, but it was only a squirrel. There were no footsteps, no sign of her brother.

Hallie returned to the cabin. Maybe Benny had crawled under the bed. He liked to hide. Perhaps he had hidden and then fallen asleep. She hadn't looked inside. She should have searched there first. Maybe she had worried for nothing. "I'm coming to get you, Benny," Hallie called. She would tickle him, and he'd laugh. She rushed into the cabin and peered under the bed. Benny wasn't there. He wasn't hiding under the table or behind the stove, either.

She went back into the woods and searched once more. Benny probably had fallen asleep and hadn't heard her. She walked along the path to the creek again, looking under bushes to see if her brother was there. When she reached the stream, she walked slowly along the creek bed. Maybe she hadn't gone far enough the first time. Benny knew he wasn't to go into the water. Still, he loved water, and sometimes he forgot. She saw a lump beside the stream. "Benny," she called and rushed forward, but it was only a gray rock.

Hallie searched for prints beside the creek. Then she

spotted a barefoot print. Had Benny been wearing his shoes? Hallie couldn't remember. The footprint was the same size as her own. Hallie was barefoot, and she wasn't sure which one of them had left the print. She knelt down hoping to see other footprints, and found one more.

"Benny!" Hallie screamed, but there was no answer. She stepped into the water and followed the stream, stopping in shallow spots to search for more footprints. If Benny had fallen into the stream, he would still be there, Hallie told herself. The water was not swift enough to carry him away. She looked for broken branches and places where he might have stopped. But there was no sign that Benny had been there.

She sat down on a log to think where he might have gone. It couldn't have been too far. His legs were short, and he couldn't run very fast. Perhaps he hadn't gone into the woods at all but had headed for the meadow instead. Hallie retraced her steps and ran back to the cabin. She looked again for Benny, hoping he had returned. But there was no sign of him.

Hallie started through the meadow, stopping at a rock outcropping. They had once taken a picnic to the spot.

Benny was frightened of it, however, because they had heard a rattlesnake. Benny was afraid of snakes and refused to go back to the rocks even after the snake had disappeared. He didn't like playing in the meadow, either. It was unlikely he would have gone there. Still, Hallie searched for the boy, calling his name, although her voice was almost gone. She spotted a clump of wildflowers. Benny loved to pick flowers to give to her or to Tessie or to Mrs. Carlson. He would hold the bouquet behind his back, then thrust it out and cry, "Surprise!" Of course the flowers were not a surprise, except to Tessie, but Hallie and Mrs. Carlson always pretended they were.

The grasses around the wildflowers had not been trampled. Hallie searched the meadow, but she had little hope that Benny would be there.

Sick with fear that something bad had happened to her brother, Hallie went back to the cabin. Tom would be home soon. He would know where to look. Hallie sat down in the doorway and put her head in her hands. Poor Benny. If he was lost, he would be frightened. What if he was calling for her, and she couldn't hear him? He might be a long way away.

She loved that little boy. All she had in the world were Benny and Tom. Mommy, Daddy, and Barbara, they all were gone. Hallie remembered when Mommy died. She had tried to explain the death to Benny. "Mommy's with Barbara in heaven," she had said.

"Where's heaven?" Benny had asked.

Hallie pointed to the sky.

Benny looked up and waved. "Hi, Mommy."

"She won't be back," Hallie explained.

Benny had frowned at that and thought for a while. Hallie wondered if he understood. Then Benny had smiled and said, "You're Mommy, Hallie."

And so she had been. She had been as much a mother to Benny as if he really had been her child. And she loved him just as fiercely.

Once a girl in Oklahoma had said, "It's too bad Barbara died instead of Benny."

"Why would you say that?" Hallie had demanded, shocked.

"Well, you know, he's not very smart."

"Do you think that matters? He's a person just like you. We love him the way he is. Maybe we love him more because he needs us."

She remembered the tree Benny had chosen at Christmas. It was funny-looking, crooked, and bare on one side, but Benny had loved it. Perhaps that was because it was different, just as he was. *Benny doesn't just need us,* Hallie thought. *We need him.*

As she recalled that tree, Hallie put her head down on her knees and began to sob. Benny needed her now more than ever. *He's lost, and I'm not there to help him.*

She cried harder and didn't stop until she felt a hand on her shoulder. "Benny?" she said, looking up quickly.

"It's me, Tom. What's the matter? Are you hurt?"

"Oh, Tom, Benny's gone! He was here when I was washing the quilts. He was helping me at first. I was so busy, and when I looked around for him he wasn't here."

"Have you searched for him?"

"I've looked all afternoon. I went through the woods and along the stream, and I even went to the meadow. I got back just a few minutes ago."

"What about the road?"

"You know he's afraid of the road. We've told him so many times how dangerous it is. He'd never go there by himself for fear of a car running him down."

"I'll look for him. You stay here in case he comes back."

Hallie nodded. She listened as Tom went into the woods, calling, "Benny! Where are you, Ben? Hallie has supper ready!" She listened until she could not hear Tom's voice any longer. She went inside and lit a fire in the cook stove. She mixed up batter for pancakes. Then she took down a jar of blackberries that Mrs. Carlson had given her.

"Save it for something special," Mrs. Carlson had said. What was more special than Benny coming home safe?

Benny didn't come home safe, however. He didn't come home at all. Tom searched through the night, coming back to the cabin from time to time to see if Benny had returned. Hallie tried to sleep, but she was jerked awake every time she heard a noise. She finally gave up napping and sat in the doorway, staring out at the stars until the sky lightened in the east. When Tom returned, she looked at him hopefully. He shook his head.

"Maybe he went to the Carlsons'," Tom said as the sun

came up. He sat in the doorway drinking a cup of coffee. Hallie had ground the coffee beans, and the coffee was fresh. Tom deserved it after his long night of looking for their brother.

"You worked at the Carlsons' yesterday. He wasn't there then. You know he won't go out on the road alone. That's the only way to get there. Besides, if he had gone to their place, the Carlsons would have brought him home, even in the middle of the night. They'd know how worried we'd be."

Tom nodded. "I don't know where else to look," he said. He squeezed Hallie's hand. She knew he was as frightened as she was.

"I'll go see the Carlsons," she said. "You've been up all night. You lie down. I'll wake you as soon as I get back."

Tom protested, but Hallie insisted. She jumped up and ran as fast as she could down the road to the Carlson farm.

Mrs. Carlson was taking down sheets from the clothesline. She removed two clothespins from her mouth and said, "I was too tired to bring in the washing last night. I didn't think I had to worry it would rain." She smiled as she folded a sheet and dropped it into a basket. Then she looked at Hallie sharply. "Why are you here so early? Is something wrong?"

"Is Benny here?" Hallie asked, gasping for breath because she had been running so hard.

Mrs. Carlson dropped the clothespins into a bag hanging on the line. "What, Benny? No, he's not here." She frowned. "Is he missing?"

"He disappeared yesterday. Tom looked for him all night. We thought maybe he came here."

"Swede!" Mrs. Carlson called. Her husband came out of the house, letting the screen door bang. "Benny's missing. See if he's in the barn. Hallie, you look in the chicken coop."

Hallie started off, clutching her side because it hurt from running.

"Wait," Mrs. Carlson called. "Maybe Tessie will have some idea." She called into the house for Tessie. The little girl came outside, and Mrs. Carlson asked, "Have you seen Benny?"

Tessie shook her head.

"What about yesterday."

Tessie shook her head again.

Like Benny, Tessie sometimes mixed up days, so Hallie wasn't sure Tessie would have remembered. Still, if he had been at the Carlson farm, Mrs. Carlson would have seen him.

Mr. Carlson came back from the barn, shaking his head. "I checked the chicken coop, too. There's no sign of him."

Hallie thanked them, then said, "I better get back. Tom and I will start looking again."

"Well, you're not going to do it alone. We'll get up a search party," Mr. Carlson said.

"A search party?" Hallie asked.

"You bet. There's a little boy missing. Folks will want to help."

"Help *us*?"

"You're the ones whose kid is missing."

"Swede, you go on over to the cabin and get started. Hallie, come inside with me, and we'll call the sheriff," Mrs. Carlson said. She turned away but not before Hallie saw her put the corner of her apron to her eye, wiping away a tear. "That dear little boy. We'll find him."

Hallie followed the woman into the house. Mrs. Carlson went to the telephone, which was mounted on the wall. It was a big brown wooden box with a speaking tube and a receiver that Mrs. Carlson held to her ear. She turned the crank to call the operator. There was a harsh grinding sound, then someone came on the line. "Gladys? That you?" Mrs.

Carlson asked. "Get me the sheriff." She waited a minute, then said, "Sheriff Eagles? The Turner boy's missing. The younger one, Benny. Hallie and Tom looked all night for him. Swede's going over there now, but you better get up a search party." She paused for a moment, then said, "That'll be fine. I'll have Gladys alert everybody. Gladys, you still on the line? Tell folks to get over to our hired man's place to look for the boy."

Mrs. Carlson hung up the receiver, then she turned to Hallie. "The sheriff said he'll be right out. Other folks will be coming, too. You run on to the cabin. Tessie and I will come over later." She bit her lip. "That is, if Benny hasn't come home by then." Mrs. Carlson put her hand to her forehead and looked away. Then she said, "We'll find him, honey. Don't you worry. We'll find him."

Home

*H*allie ran back down the road to the cabin. Just as she got there, a car pulled off at the cabin. "You find Mr. Benny yet, did you?" Sheriff Eagles asked.

"No, sir." Suddenly Hallie began to cry. She put her hands over her face, but the tears spilled out. She thought of the foxes and coyotes and snakes out there, the rocks Benny could fall over, and the streams. She should have done a better job of watching him. She wiped the tears from her face, embarrassed.

"Now, sis, don't you worry none. We'll find Mr. Benny."

"How? There are so many places he could be."

"And so many folks will be out looking." The sheriff

opened the car door and swung around, holding on to the door frame to push himself out.

The passenger door opened, and Jimmy Watson from school jumped out. He grinned at Hallie. "The sheriff saw me by the filling station and told me to come along. We aren't the only ones searching for your brother." He pointed at two cars, then stepped out into the road and waved them to a stop.

A man Hallie didn't know got out of one car, while another boy from school and his father opened the doors of the second one. Before long, more than a dozen men and boys had gathered beside the cabin, listening to the sheriff's instructions about where to search. "We'll set up things here. Maybe the boy will come back on his own," the sheriff said. "Now we got to decide who's to search where."

I ought to fix them coffee, Hallie thought. She didn't have much. She'd have to stretch it, but it was the least she could do. "I'll make coffee," she whispered to the sheriff.

"Don't you worry about that, sis. Coffee's coming. You tell these men about Benny."

Hallie told them her brother was friendly, but he would be scared if he heard someone strange calling him. "He might not answer. If you think you see him, yell that you've found Bob. Bob was our rabbit," she said.

The men were assigned areas to search—the woods, the meadow, the fields, the roadside. Then the sheriff gave each man a whistle. "That's our way," he explained to Hallie. "Somebody blows a whistle, it means the boy's found."

The men were about to leave when another car stopped, and a man got out, followed by Dan and Harold. *The man must be Dan's father*, Hallie thought. *What were they doing there?* Surely they weren't going to search for Benny. But why else would they have come?

Tom saw the two boys, too, and stared. Then he went over and held out his hand. "We sure do appreciate you helping," he said.

"Tom," Harold said.

"Tom," Dan repeated.

Another car drove up and parked by the cabin, and Mrs. Powell got out with a big coffee boiler. Hallie helped her carry it inside, where they added wood to the coals in the cook stove and then set the boiler on top. "I brought cups, too," Mrs. Powell told Hallie, setting a dozen tin cups on the table.

A few minutes later a woman arrived with a plate of fried doughnuts. "I made them for breakfast, but when the call come, my husband got right up from the table and started over here to help look for the boy. So I brung the doughnuts, too." Then she said, "There's others coming. We'll have dinner ready when the men get back."

Hallie sat down on the bed. She had been up all night and had never been so tired. "You rest," Mrs. Carlson said. She had arrived with Tessie. "Tessie knows Benny is missing, and she wants to help find him, too."

"I brought Ragman," Tessie said, holding up her Raggedy Ann doll. "She'll find Benny." Then she called, "Benny, you come here right now."

Hallie didn't want to sleep. It wouldn't be right. So many others were looking for her brother. Still, when Mrs. Carlson insisted, Hallie lay down on the bed. She closed her eyes for just a moment. When she awoke, the sun was high in the sky. "Benny?" she asked, sitting up. "Did they find Benny?"

"I'm sorry. Not yet," a woman told her. "They're still looking. They won't give up till they find him."

Hallie glanced out the open door. The sheriff was still there along with several men. "I shouldn't have slept," she said.

"Best thing for you. Besides, there's plenty of us here." The woman pointed to the foot of the bed. "I brung in the quilts you left drying in the bushes. Men don't think of such things." Hallie had forgotten all about the quilts that she had washed the day before. *Was it only yesterday?* she wondered.

The cabin was full of women. Several were gathered around the table, which was crowded with pies and cookies and cakes. Three girls were making sandwiches. One of them was Wilma! Hallie stared at her. She was spreading butter on a slice of bread as she chatted with Cathy. She turned and grinned at Hallie.

"Wilma?" Hallie said, standing up. She didn't understand. Why would Wilma have come to help?

"Hi." Wilma set down the bread and went over to Hallie. "I know you don't like me much, but I wanted to do what I could. I think your little brother's dear. He made me smile when he wanted to sing 'Happy Days' at Christmas."

"I thought *you* didn't like *me,*" Hallie said.

Wilma frowned. "What gave you that idea? I thought it was swell you and your brothers could live together like you do." She glanced around until she spotted a woman Hallie assumed was her mother. She lowered her voice. "I would give anything to do that, but I don't think I'd have the nerve. I mean, it's really something that you can get along without *adults*. You always seem so sure of yourself." She glanced away. "I was a little afraid of you."

"But you called us squatters."

"I guess that's because I was jealous of you. I wanted to hurt you. I really didn't mean it, and I'm sorry I said it. Heck, my grandfather squatted here fifty years ago. Right now, we're just all neighbors." She pointed outside.

Hallie went to the door and saw several boys from her class sitting among the men who were eating the sandwiches the girls had made. They smiled at Hallie. "We'll find him," one said. He gave her a thumbs-up.

"I know," Hallie replied. She went outside and sat down on a log and put her head into her hands. Surely with all these people looking, someone would find Benny. She sniffed back tears. She didn't want people to see her cry. She had to be brave, like Tom. He had come in with the men but was getting ready to go out again.

"I'm sorry you're sad." Wilma had come out of the cabin and sat down next to Hallie. "I just know they'll find your brother."

Hallie was glad Wilma hadn't asked her where Benny might be. People had been asking her that since they arrived. How would she know? If she did, she would have searched there for Benny herself. "My sister ran off once," Wilma continued. "Dad found her in the chicken coop. She was sitting on an egg. She was trying to hatch it."

Despite herself, Hallie smiled.

The men finished eating. Hallie thought they would go home then. After all, they had planting and milking and other chores to do. Instead of getting into their cars, however, the men readied themselves to go back out to search for Benny.

Nobody paid any attention to a truck going fast down the road toward town until the driver honked. Hallie recognized the truck. It delivered baked goods to the store in town every other day. The bread truck came to a stop, and a man got out. "Anybody here lose a little boy?" he called.

Hallie jumped up. "Did you find Benny? He's my brother. Where is he?"

Women came out of the house, and men stopped what they were doing to stare. The bread man hurried to the other side of the truck and opened the door. Benny leaped out. "Hi, Hallie. I have bread." He held a half-eaten piece of bread in his hand.

Hallie rushed to her brother, tears streaming down her face. "I'm so glad you're safe!" she said.

Tom ran up behind Hallie and lifted Benny in his arms. "We missed you, Ben!" Then the three of them hugged each other.

"Hi, Benny," Tessie said, hurrying toward her friend. "I brought Ragman."

Benny squirmed to get down.

"Where you been, son?" the sheriff asked. He smiled at Benny. Behind him, the others clapped. Someone blew a whistle several times, the signal to the men still searching that Benny had been found.

"I went to sleep," Benny said.

"Where'd you find him?" the sheriff asked the bread man.

"Funniest thing. He was sitting in the middle of the road talking to a rabbit. Rabbit just stayed there when I stopped, didn't even hop off."

"Where was that?"

"Must have been three, four miles up the road."

"How do you suppose he got so far?" the sheriff asked. "We never thought to look way up there."

"He must have been chasing Bob," Hallie said.

"Bob. Oh yeah. I guess that's what he was calling the rabbit," the bread man told her. "I thought he was saying 'job,' but it must have been 'Bob,' with a 'B.'"

Benny thought that over for a minute. "'B' for 'Bob,'" he said. "Hey, Tessie, 'B' for 'Bob.'"

"'B' for 'Benny.' We have cake," Tessie replied.

"Oh boy!" Benny took off for the cabin.

"Well, sis, you got your boy back," the sheriff said. "I expect all you needed was a bread man."

"Maybe we needed everybody," Hallie said softly. Tom nodded in agreement.

Hallie looked at the people who had come to search. They had gathered around Benny when he got out of the truck, but now they were packing up. Those who had heard the whistle were coming in from the woods and the fields, asking if Benny was all right.

Several men slapped the bread man on the back. He was embarrassed and said he had to get back to his deliveries. "All's I did was stop for a kid."

"You come by the office and pick up the reward," the sheriff told him.

"The what?" the man asked.

Hallie heard the words and frowned. No one had mentioned a reward. She and Tom hadn't even thought about one.

"It's twenty-five dollars. Old Man Morton put it up. Dangdest thing. I thought he was the cheapest man in the county. Harold said it was his dad's idea, too." The sheriff shook his head.

Tom began moving through the crowd and thanking people. So did Hallie.

"Ain't nothing to thank us for. You'd have done the same for us," one man said.

Another man shrugged and told Tom, "Glad the boy's safe."

Wilma had started for a car with her mother. Now she stopped beside Hallie.

"Thank you," Hallie said. "I'm glad we talked."

"Me too. Do you think sometime I could come over and maybe you could help me with my arithmetic? You're the smartest one in the class."

"Sure," Hallie said and smiled at the girl. "Maybe you'd help me with grammar."

"See you at school," Wilma said as she closed the car door.

The sheriff, too, got into his car and drove off. Before long, only the Carlsons remained. Mrs. Carlson hugged Hallie. She'd never done that before. Hallie hugged her back. "I'm so glad . . . ," Mrs. Carlson said and stopped to wipe the tears from her cheeks.

"I can't believe all these people just showed up. We don't even know half of them," Hallie said.

"You're their neighbors. That's what neighbors do."

Mr. Carlson slapped Tom on the back. "I was thinking it's about time we done some work on that old cabin of yours, maybe add a room. I think we got an extra bed up to the house, too. No need for anybody to sleep on the floor."

Hallie stared at Mr. Carlson when he called the place *their* cabin. "I thought you were going to tear it down one day," she said.

"I thought I was, too, but now that we've got good folks living in it, it'd be a shame to put them out. You folks are family. The place is yours as long as you want it. We expect you'll be here for a long time. Other people around here, they think smartly of you. I hope after today, you know that."

Tom and Hallie exchanged a long look. "Thanks, Mr. Carlson," Tom said.

"'Bout time you started calling me Swede."

Tessie skipped along beside her mother on the way to the Carlsons' car. "See you tomorrow," Tessie called. She waved Raggedy Ann's hand.

"Okay," Benny said. He turned to Hallie. "I had cake, but I'm still hungry."

"People left enough food for a week," Hallie told Tom.

The three of them watched the Carlsons' car go down the road, sending up a spray of dirt. Dust devils danced in the road. Birds sang, and wildflowers waved in the breeze. Benny began to sing "Happy Days."

"You still think we ought to go on to California?" Hallie asked.

Tom shook his head. "How about you?"

Hallie smiled at him as she took Benny's hand. "We don't have to. We're home."

Glossary

Bread lines: During the Great Depression, government and charity workers handed out free food to poor people, who waited in long lines to receive it.

Carpet sweeper: An appliance with a broom handle and a case containing rotating bristles. When run over a rug, it picks up such things as crumbs and dog hair.

Cartwheel: A silver dollar. Until about 1950, silver dollars were often used instead of paper dollars.

Continent: One of seven principle land masses on the earth. They are North America, South America, Antarctica, Europe, Asia, Africa, and Australia.

Cook stove: A cast-iron stove in which a wood fire is used to cook or heat food.

Dinner bell: A large, loud bell mounted outside a house, rung when meals are ready or in case of an emergency.

Dust Bowl: In the 1930s, a drought caused land in America's midsection to dry up and blow away. Winds carried the dust as far east as the Atlantic Ocean.

Dusted out: A phrase describing farmers who went broke and had to move away from their land during the Dust Bowl.

Dust pneumonia: Winds during the Dust Bowl stirred up fine dust that got into people's lungs, causing illness.

Essex Terraplane Deluxe Eight: A powerful automobile made by the Hudson Motor Car Company in the 1930s.

Feed sack: Animal feed was sold in cheap fabric sacks that were often printed with flowers, animals, geometrics, and other designs. Women made the sacks into clothing, curtains, and tablecloths.

Flivver: An old car in poor condition.

Great Depression: A severe worldwide economic downturn in the 1930s. Banks failed, factories closed, and millions of people lost their jobs.

Hobo: A tramp or vagrant. In the 1930s, many men who had lost their jobs wandered the country as hobos looking for work.

Icebox: A wooden cabinet with a compartment for ice. The box was used to keep food cold. Ice men in wagons or trucks sold ice to replace what had melted.

Lincoln Logs: Notched miniature logs used to construct doll-size cabins, forts, and other buildings.

Mercantile: A general store.

Migrant: A person who moves from one location to another, often in search of a better life.

Model T: A popular automobile made by the Ford Motor Company from 1908 to 1927.

Old Dutch cleanser: A pumice-based scouring powder.

Persian pickle: Paisley. Feed sacks were often printed with paisley designs.

Pie safe: A cabinet, usually with punched tin or screen inserts, used for storage. Hot pies are placed in the safe, where the inserts keep out flies but allow air to circulate and cool the pastry.

Ragbag: A sack that contains old clothes or bits of material salved for mending, quilting, or other uses.

Rumble seat: An uncovered passenger seat that opens out from the back of a car.

Soddy: A house made from strips of prairie grass stacked one on top of another.

Squatter: A person who settles illegally on someone else's land.

Tin Lizzie: A Model T Ford, also known as Leaping Lena.

Acknowledgments

My parents, Harriett and Forrest Dallas, were married in Illinois in 1933, in the midst of the Great Depression. Shortly afterward, Dad lost his job as a floor walker at a Kresge's dime store in Moline. He took Mom back to Harveyville, Kansas, to live with his parents and help Grandma and Grandpa Dallas on the farm. That summer, a neighbor agreed to pay him a dollar for a day's work in the fields. Dad worked so hard that he finished up by noon and earned just fifty cents. That was the only money he made all summer.

I was raised with my parents' stories of the "dirty thirties"—of the dust storms blowing away the top soil and of desperate families driving along the dirt roads in beat-up cars, looking for work. There were also tales of farm women gathered in the shade of trumpet vines for quiltings, of picnics with relatives, of neighbors helping neighbors. Mom never forgot the hardship of that summer, but she also told me 1933 was one of the happiest years of her life. Times were tough, but Mom and Dad had family. And a home.

Thanks, Mom and Dad, for all those stories, and thank you, Barb McNally, senior children's editor at Sleeping Bear Press, for helping me tell them. Thanks to my agent, Danielle Egan-Miller, and to my family—Bob, Dana, Kendal, Lloyd, and Forrest. This Kansas story is your heritage, too.

Sandra Dallas

Sandra Dallas is the *New York Times*–bestselling author of the middle-grade novels *Hardscrabble*, *The Quilt Walk*, and *Red Berries, White Clouds, Blue Sky*. She has written ten nonfiction books and fifteen adult novels, including *The Last Midwife*, *Prayers for Sale*, *The Diary of Mattie Spenser*, and *The Persian Pickle Club*. A former Denver bureau chief for *Business Week* magazine, she is the recipient of three National Cowboy & Western Heritage Museum Wrangler awards, three Western Writers of America Spur Awards, and four Women Writing the West WILLA Awards. She lives in Denver. Visit her at www.sandradallas.com.